BUILDING DREAMS

Joyce Byers Hill

Lilac Hill Publishing

Yakima, WA

Books by Joyce Byers Hill

A PLACE CALLED HOPE series:

Diamond in the Rough

JC's Hope

Building Dreams

Dedication

I would like to dedicate this book to my sister Jean, who read my first two novels so many times she insisted she needed a third book in the series.

I also dedicate this book to my daughter Chereé, without whose constant encouragement it never would have made it past the first chapter. It was fun brainstorming with you, Chereé. I'm sure the story is better than it would have been without your input.

And to my readers, I hope you have been enjoying your trips to A Place Called Hope. If you keep returning, I'll keep writing. Invite your friends to visit A Place Called Hope. You know you want to.

Chapter One

Aiden Byers stood with his hands in the front pockets of his Levis, staring across the lot at the beginnings of a new house. Even though no walls had been constructed yet, he knew that was on today's agenda. He smiled as he thought of the interesting twist his life had taken. He always knew he and his cousin Kaci would eventually take over running Byers Construction, but he never dreamed he would also be building houses on the side. Before returning home from the Army, his extensive building experience had been projects on a much larger scale. While stationed with the Army Corps of Engineers, his days were filled with constructing roads, bridges, dams, and airfields. Building houses required a different skill set. One he eagerly learned from his aunt and uncle.

Aiden's uncle, Travis Harmon, was the pastor at Hope Community Church. He was also a closet carpenter, having previously built several custom homes. His Aunt Meghan was his dad's only sibling. Meghan grew up alongside her younger brother Todd in the family construction business started by their father. When Aiden's grandfather passed away, Todd and Meghan took over the family business. Like her brother, Meghan was not only a skilled carpenter but an expert heavy equipment operator. Although Aiden's aunt had only built one custom home, it was flawless. In fact, his aunt and uncle met while she was operating a bulldozer on the property where she would build what would become their home.

No one would ever say Aiden's family was typical. All the kids in the family, beginning with his dad and Aunt Meghan, grew up climbing around on heavy equipment. They all learned how to operate a Bobcat before they learned to drive. While their friends seemed content playing with Tonka trucks, the kids in this family cut their teeth on the real thing.

Kaci, being the oldest cousin by several years, didn't spend much time on heavy equipment anymore. She had a very full life with her husband and nine-year-old twins. The twins, Aaron and Sophie, became the third generation of kids to grow up climbing around on the company Bobcats. In addition to being a full-time mom to active nine-year-olds, Kaci was managing the business end of JC's Hope, the youth center started by her brother Josh. Now, she was also being groomed to take over the bookkeeping end of Byers Construction, while Aiden was learning the ropes to take over the actual construction portion of the business.

Of the four Byers and Harmon cousins, Kaci and Aiden were the two who never strayed far from the family construction business. They had both been involved in the business in one way or another since they were teenagers. So, there was never a question of who would take the reins once Todd and Meghan decided to step back a bit. Kaci's brother Josh, better known as JC, never had a burning passion for construction. His heart and soul belonged to music, and his calling was helping troubled kids. He combined those two loves when he opened JC's Hope. Kaci and JC's younger sister Ryleigh seemed to be a happy mix of her older siblings. She loved the construction company that was entering its third generation, but deep down she had an artist's heart. In her final year of college as a graphic design major, she was still exploring her career options.

As Aiden continued to marvel at the construction project in front of him, he thanked God for his close-knit family. He saw the way the entire family rallied behind JC after his near-fatal car accident and was a source of never-ending support in his quest to open a youth center. Once the center was open, many of the kids who passed through the doors became like family. In fact, some became family in every sense of the word. JC met his wife Amy and her younger brother Matt because of the center. When Aiden's dad took Matt under his wing as an apprentice at the construction company while he was a teenager, Matt became the little brother Aiden never had.

Matt had been working at the construction company full-time since he graduated from high school two years earlier. He was a quick learner and eagerly soaked up all the training he could get from Todd and Aiden. When Matt expressed an interest in building houses someday, he and Aiden decided to make it a joint venture. The two young men approached their family with the idea and weren't surprised at the overwhelming support they received. After telling their family they wanted the first house to be a gift to newlyweds JC and Amy, everyone offered their complete support. Todd and Meghan, as owners of Byers Construction, insisted on donating the building supplies. Since Travis hoped to be able to cut back on his church responsibilities once he found an associate pastor, he would have more free time on his hands. He planned to fill some of that free time by offering his carpentry skills to help with the project.

Aiden stood transfixed by the early morning sunrise over the construction site and thanked God for the five-acre parcel next to his aunt and uncle's house that went on the market just as they were searching for property. It never ceased to amaze him how easily God seemed to make all the puzzle pieces fall into place.

Once Aiden and Matt had both gotten a taste for constructing buildings and discussed the idea of building a house for JC and Amy, things seemed to come together faster than they could think of the next step.

Aiden didn't hear the Ford Ranger pickup pull onto the property. Matt had already climbed out of the truck and walked up to Aiden, waiting with a smile to be noticed. Still lost in thought, Aiden turned in Matt's direction and was shocked to see the tall young man standing a few feet away.

The two men, who shared a deep brotherly bond, laughed simultaneously. Aiden shook his head as Matt reached out to shake his hand.

"Bro," Matt said as he patted Aiden on the back. "You were sure deep in thought about something."

Aiden grinned as he replied, "Are you as excited as I am to start on the walls today?"

"Oh, yeah! I can't wait to get started. Working on some of those commercial buildings was a lot of fun, but this house…" Matt's voice trailed off as he looked at the foundation and subfloors just waiting to become a house.

"I hear you, Matt," Aiden quickly agreed. "This first house is going to be special. Dad's coming over to help this morning, isn't he?"

"Yeah," Matt confirmed. "We left the house at the same time this morning, but he said he needed to stop at the shop first. I think Travis is going to help today too."

Before his sister had married JC, Matt and Amy had shared an apartment. After the wedding, Matt moved into Aiden's old room at Todd and Nicole's. Todd was like a father to Matt, having easily stepped into that role shortly after they met, and Todd learned what Matt's home life had been like. Even though Matt and Amy's parents had successfully completed rehab and had been clean and sober for a couple of years, their relationship was still shaky.

"Hey, Aiden," Matt began, "can I ask you something before Todd and Travis get here?"

"Sure," Aiden replied. "What's up?"

Matt kicked the toe of his work boot into the dirt before speaking. It was a habit Aiden had noticed whenever Matt was nervous.

"You know my dad hasn't worked in several years, right?"

"Yeah," Aiden acknowledged. "That's tough."

"I thought once he finished rehab, he would get a job. He's been clean since right before I graduated, but it doesn't seem like he's made much of an effort to find a job. I think he got so used to not working, that I'm not sure he really wants to change."

"That's a hard transition, Matt," Aiden said as he nodded in understanding. "I'm sure it's easier to just continue with the status quo than to try to change."

"I was wondering," Matt continued, kicking his boot into the dirt again. "What do you think about hiring him to help on the house? You know, as a laborer, to help with some of the basics? He's not a skilled carpenter or anything. He's never done any of that type of work. But maybe some of the extra stuff that needs to be done. Maybe carrying lumber and helping to hold walls when they're being braced. That kind of thing."

"You know, Matt," Aiden agreed with a smile, "that's not a bad idea. There's always stuff to be done around the construction site that he could do. And it might go a long way to boosting his confidence. Maybe he just needs a push in the right direction. Why don't we run it by Dad and Uncle Travis when they get here and see what they think?"

"I don't even know if my dad would agree to it," Matt said. "But I thought it might be worth a try."

"I agree," Aiden said, pointing toward the road. "There's Dad and Uncle Travis now."

Travis pulled his pickup onto the property right behind Todd's company truck. The two men, still physically fit in their early 60s, shook hands as they started toward the younger men.

"Well, boys," Travis greeted, "are you ready to build some walls?"

"You bet!" Matt said with excitement. "I can't wait to get started!"

"Dad," Aiden began as he shook hands with his uncle Travis. "Matt just had a great idea. What do you guys think of hiring his dad to help around the construction site? You know, odd jobs, carrying lumber, helping to brace walls, cleanup, that kind of thing. I think it might boost his confidence and ease him back into the working world."

Todd looked at Travis before cautiously agreeing. "I think it might work. Do you know if he's still sober and attending his AA meetings? We certainly can't, and won't, tolerate drinking on the job site."

"It's been a week or so since I've talked to John," Travis answered. "But I'm pretty sure he's still on the right track. Have you seen anything to indicate otherwise, Matt?"

"No," Matt replied. "You know our relationship still isn't great, but I see him once in a while and he seems okay."

"I say we give him a try," Travis suggested. "We'll just keep an eye on him, and if it doesn't work out, we cut him loose."

"I trust your instincts," Todd agreed hesitantly. "Matt, why don't you talk to him and see if he's willing to work with us? He needs to know the ground rules. If you want, I'll go with you to talk to him."

"Thanks, guys," Matt replied. "I'll swing by and talk to him tonight and see if he's even interested."

"Well, gentlemen," Aiden said, "why don't we slap on some hard hats and start building walls?"

"Let's go!" Matt yelled with youthful excitement.

Before long, sawhorses and tools were set up on the subfloors, and the sound of power saws and hammers filled the air.

Chapter Two

Matt parked his pickup in front of his dad and mom's house, then simply sat there staring at the house. *Maybe this wasn't my best idea,* he thought to himself. "Well," he said out loud, "I guess there's only one way to find out." He climbed out of his truck and started walking up the sidewalk toward the front door.

Even though this was the house where he grew up, he didn't feel comfortable simply walking in. He rang the doorbell and waited for someone to come to the door. Within a couple of minutes, the door opened, and Matt found himself face-to-face with his father.

"Well, son," John greeted, "you don't stop by very often. This must be a special visit. Come on in."

John stepped back to allow his son to enter the house. Once inside, Matt took in his surroundings and inwardly groaned. Nothing had changed. It still looked like neither of his parents made any effort to keep a tidy house. Overflowing ashtrays littered the coffee table, and fast-food containers were strewn around the kitchen. It's not like they were busy working for a living. Maybe this really wasn't a good idea. Maybe he should just visit for a few minutes and not mention the job offer.

"So," John began, "to what do I owe this surprise visit? Your mom's not here. She went to the store."

Matt didn't make a move to sit down and get comfortable, nor did his dad offer a place to sit.

"I wanted to ask you a question," Matt began. "Aiden and I are building a house for Amy and JC."

"Must be nice," John replied bitterly.

"Dad," Matt said, already exasperated, "do you want to hear what I have to say, or not?"

John sank down onto the sofa before replying. "Sorry, son. I guess old habits still die hard. Have a seat and let's talk."

Matt sat down in an overstuffed chair across from his dad. "As I said," Matt began again, "Aiden and I are building a house for Amy and JC. We're thinking of building houses on the side, in addition to working at Byers Construction. We're testing the idea by building one for Amy and JC, and we just started framing the walls. I was wondering if you might be interested in coming to work for us…maybe helping with some of the odd jobs around the construction site. You know, helping to brace up walls, moving around the tools, carrying lumber, things like that. It would give you a chance to earn some money. Are you interested in that at all?"

"I don't know, son," John replied. "I haven't done anything like that before."

"It's not difficult work, Dad. And it wouldn't be every day. Just whenever we have time to work on the house."

"Well," John replied hesitantly, "maybe."

"Okay, good," Matt said. "There's something we need to get clear before you accept the job, though. I don't see you much, but can I correctly assume you're staying sober and going to your AA meetings? If not, this isn't happening."

"Still don't have much faith in your old man, huh?"

"Well, Dad, it's not like you've given me a lot of reason to have faith in you. But I know how hard you and Mom worked in rehab, and I pray every day that you'll never throw that away. So, on that condition, do you want the job, or not?"

John sighed heavily, then reached over to shake his son's hand. "Thanks for the offer, son. And yes, I accept. When do I start?"

"We'll be working on the house part of the day tomorrow, so I'll just plan to stop by to pick you up on my way over, okay?"

When his father nodded, Matt stood to go, then turned at the door. "It's good to see you, Dad. Tell Mom I said hi. I'll see you tomorrow."

John patted his son on the back. "Thanks for stopping by son. And thanks for the job offer. You won't regret it."

"I really hope not, Dad. See you tomorrow."

* * *

The next afternoon, still not sure he had done the right thing, Matt picked up his dad and headed to the job site. They didn't talk much on the short drive, which was fine with Matt. He and his dad had been estranged most of his life, so they didn't have a lot to talk about. He had been trying to repair their damaged relationship ever since his parents made it to his high school graduation, but his dad needed to meet him halfway. Matt wasn't sure that would happen.

Matt parked his pickup next to a Byers Construction truck and climbed out, grabbing two hard hats from the seat behind him. Handing one to his dad, he said, "Everyone is required to wear a hard hat on the job site. I'll introduce you to the guys, but you probably remember most of them."

John didn't reply, simply following Matt toward the partly framed house.

Matt and his dad walked up to a small group of men who were just grabbing tools to begin work.

"Hey, guys," Matt began. "Most of you may remember my dad, John Phoenix. Dad, this is Travis, Todd, and Aiden."

John shook hands and greeted each of the men.

Matt turned to the teenager standing nearby. "Dad, this is Blake. He's one of the high school students in the apprentice program at Byers Construction. He's helping on the house in exchange for woodshop credit at school."

John shook Blake's hand, then turned to his son. "Is that the program you were involved with?"

"That's right," Matt answered with a smile. "It's a great program and helped me a lot."

Matt fastened his tool belt around his waist and started toward the house. "Well, guys, should we see how much more framing we can get done this afternoon?"

Within a few minutes, the small crew was hard at work building walls. Although he didn't appear to be overly eager to work, John did what was asked of him. He carried two-by-fours to the men building the walls, refilled their nail pouches, and helped tip up walls to be braced. All in all, it was nice to have an extra set of hands on the job site.

The afternoon flew by quickly as several more walls were added to the framework of the house. When it was time to call it a day, and the crew began gathering tools, Matt told Aiden he was going to run his dad home. Although his dad had not complained once during the afternoon, Matt was perceptive enough to see that being on task for an extended period of time was not something his dad was used to.

Once Matt drove off, and Travis left to take Blake home, Aiden walked over to help his dad finish policing the area to make sure no tools were left behind. He found his dad on the back side of the house, walking around with a trash bucket and picking things up off the ground.

When Aiden approached, Todd said, "I'm not sure it's going to work having John help on the house."

"Why do you say that, Dad? I thought he did okay." Aiden asked.

Todd reached out and showed Aiden the trash bucket. The bottom of the bucket was littered with cigarette butts.

"He's making a mess of the job site by tossing his cigarette butts everywhere," Todd said. "If he's going to smoke, it would be nice if he tossed the butts in a can instead of littering the ground."

"I agree," Aiden said, nodding. "But you're not judging him more harshly than you would someone else because of the run-ins you had with him back at the beginning, are you?"

Todd looked at his son and dropped his shoulders. "You know, son, I hadn't given that any thought. Maybe you're right. It was sure nice having the extra set of hands today. I guess a few cigarette butts aren't the end of the world. How about I take you out to Luigi's for dinner? Your mom's working at the hospital tonight, so I'm on my own."

"Pizza sounds good to me, Dad," Aiden agreed. "Do you want me to text Matt and have him meet us at Luigi's after he drops his dad off?"

"That's a great idea. I'm sure he's hungry. The boy sure knows how to put in a hard day's work."

* * *

Todd and Aiden had just placed their pizza order and settled into a booth when Matt arrived. Aiden caught his eye and waved him over to join them.

As Matt sat down, he said, "Sorry I bailed before all the cleanup was done. I could tell Dad was more than ready to call it a day. Before I got your text, I was going to swing back by the job site and clean up Dad's cigarette butts. I noticed he had been just tossing them on the ground. Sorry about that."

"Matt," Todd said, "your dad's actions are not a reflection of you or your character. Don't worry about going back over. I cleaned the butts up before we left."

"Thanks, Todd," Matt replied with relief. "I guess I'll have to talk to Dad and hope he listens."

"That's not a 'today' problem, Matt," Todd said. "Ah, just in time. Here comes the pizza."

For the next half hour, the men enjoyed their pizza as they wound down for the day.

Todd leaned back in his chair, with a look of satisfaction on his face. "I never get tired of Luigi's pizza.

"So, guys," Todd continued, "how do you think it's going with working two jobs? You both put in solid time at the shop and somehow manage to keep making progress on the house. Do you think you'll burn yourselves out?"

Aiden and Matt looked at each other and grinned.

Matt spoke first. "I can't speak for Aiden, but I don't see a problem. It's almost as if one job fuels the other. And both jobs are satisfying. It's just a different kind of satisfaction with each job. I don't know quite how to explain it. Working at Byers Construction is like having a good solid base. It's satisfying work, and there's always something new to learn. I love learning how to operate all the heavy equipment. That's not available on the house project. But the house is satisfying in a completely different way. It's like we're our own bosses and we get to make decisions that affect the design of the house. A house that our family will be living in. That makes it very special."

"I agree with Matt," Aiden said, nodding. "I couldn't have said it any better."

"So," Todd began, "once this first project house is finished, do you think you'll want to continue building houses, knowing it will be a second job?"

"I know I want to," Matt said, without giving it another thought.

"Me too," Aiden added. "Matt and I work very well together. I could easily see it being a side venture we would really enjoy."

"Somehow," Todd said with a smile, "I knew that would be your answer. Well, boys, what say we call it a day?"

"Right behind you," Aiden said in agreement.

"I need to stop and get gas, Todd," Matt said. "But I'll be home right after that."

The three men headed to their trucks, satisfied they had all put in a good day, and were more than ready to kick back and relax.

Chapter Three

When Travis walked into the gym at JC's Hope, he was not surprised to find it empty. It was early afternoon, and the center normally didn't get busy until after school let out for the day. As he worked his way down the hall, he heard music coming from one of the rooms and suspected that would be where he would find his son. He stopped outside the door to the music room, leaned against the wall, and simply soaked in the sounds. His mind went back to the day a few months after Josh's accident when he was surprised to see his son seated at the piano at home for the first time since the accident. No one in the family, including Josh, thought they would ever hear that beautiful music again. During a brief lull in the music, Travis opened the door and walked into the room.

"Is that another new song you're working on, son?" Travis asked as he walked over and sat beside Josh on the piano bench.

Josh smiled as he replied. "I didn't hear you come in, Dad. Yeah, I've been working on it for a few days. This song seems to be coming easier than some of them."

"Maybe because you're a lot more relaxed these days," Travis suggested. "Enjoy it while you can. Before you know it, your life is going to get mighty busy. Speaking of which, how is

Amy feeling these days? I haven't seen her for about a week."

Thinking about his pregnant wife always made Josh happy. There was a time when he thought he'd never be blessed with a family. But God had other plans. He and Amy have been married for a couple years and are expecting their first child in a few months.

"She's doing great," Josh replied happily. "She had a doctor's appointment earlier this week and the doctor said everything looks fine. She's past the morning sickness too, so that makes her very happy."

"I'm sure it does," Travis said with a chuckle. "I remember your mom having some very strong opinions about the morning sickness phase."

Travis stood and started toward the door. "I stopped by because I wanted to chat with you for a minute before you get busy this afternoon."

"Did you want to talk in the office, Dad?"

"I don't want to take up a lot of your time," Travis replied. "Let's walk and talk. You know I've been planning to hire an associate pastor at the church so I can start stepping back a bit. I want to eventually kind of semi-retire so I have time to help Matt and Aiden with their house-building venture. And, of course, have time to spoil grandkids."

Josh chuckled as he replied, "Well, of course."

"Anyway, I just wanted to let you know I've started advertising for the position. So, if you happen to hear of someone who might be qualified, and a good fit for Hope, let me know. Otherwise, I'll just see what kind of candidates the job listing pulls in."

"I'll be sure to keep my ears open," Josh said. "Good luck. I know you won't have any trouble filling your semi-retirement days."

"That's what I hear," Travis laughed. "Mike told me the other day he doesn't know how he had time to work. He's busier since he semi-retired than he ever was working full time!"

Travis had barely mentioned his name when Mike Slater walked in the front door.

Mike was Josh's benefactor who gifted him the warehouse and property for the youth center. He was a constant supporter of JC's Hope, always eager to make sure the center had everything the kids could possibly need or want.

Josh and Travis walked up and shook Mike's hand as he perused the bulletin board for the latest happenings at the center. The bulletin board is where Mike got a lot of his ideas for things the center may need.

"How are you doing, Mike?" Travis asked.

"Just fine, Travis," Mike replied. Then he looked at JC with a grin. "I see Kyle still hasn't beaten my top score in the baseball game."

JC laughed as he replied, "No, you're still a legend here, Mike."

Mike chuckled while warming up one of the arcade games he supplied to the center. "I've got to keep practicing. Some of these younger kids might beat me!"

Travis slapped Mike on the back, then said, "I won't keep you from your game, Maestro! Hey, I wanted to let you know I just started advertising for an associate pastor. So, if you know of anyone who would be a good fit, let me know. I'm in no special hurry to fill the position. I just want to make sure whoever I find is qualified and understands small-town churches."

"Okay, Travis," Mike replied without taking his eyes off the game. "I'll give it some thought and keep my ears open."

"Thanks, Mike," Turning to Josh, Travis said, "Well, I'm going to head over to the church and get some work done. Be sure to give Amy a hug for me when you get home tonight."

"I will, Dad. Tell Mom I said hi."

"Will do," Travis replied as he headed out the door.

* * *

Bailey Campbell sat at her desk, staring out the window of her fourth-floor apartment at the hordes of people scurrying along on the sidewalks below. Other than her four-year stint in the Army, she had spent several years living in the Seattle metro area, but still couldn't adapt to city life. *I'm just not made for city life,* she thought to herself. *It's like trying to fit a square peg into a round hole. I miss small-town living.*

Bailey, her twin brothers, and their younger sister had grown up on a dairy farm just south of the Canadian border. Her family had relocated to Seattle several years ago when her dad began working as a software developer for Microsoft. After creating a program for the dairy industry, Microsoft began wooing him to join their development team. Her brothers, Wyatt and Spencer, both gamers and self-proclaimed computer geeks, took to the fast pace of city life like they were born for it. They both went to work for Microsoft right out of college. Her little sister Emma shared her dislike for the city, though. She enjoyed some of the fun things to do, as well as the opportunities Seattle offered, but preferred a slower pace.

Since Bailey's discharge from the Army, the girls had been sharing an apartment while they completed their college degrees. After serving as a Chaplain Assistant in the Army, Bailey returned to college to get her Master of Divinity degree. She earned her degree about the same time Emma completed her Bachelor of Business Administration degree. Now they were both actively searching for jobs.

With a sigh, Bailey ran her hands through her shoulder-length hair and turned back to her computer where she had a page of job listings open. There were several listings for senior pastors and interim pastors in the greater Seattle area, but she just couldn't get excited about any of them.

"Emma," Bailey began, looking at her sister sprawled out on the sofa with her laptop, "are you finding any jobs that look exciting?"

Emma closed the lid of her laptop with frustration. Though they were very different in appearance, the sisters had similar temperaments and loved sharing an apartment. Bailey was tall and had dark curly hair, while Emma was a few inches shorter than her sister and had long straight blonde hair.

"There are all kinds of potential jobs, and a lot of them have incredible starting salaries," Emma replied. "But most of them are in Seattle and the surrounding area."

Bailey chuckled as she replied, "You do realize we live in 'Seattle and the surrounding area,' right?"

Emma stood and walked over to her sister's desk and pulled up a chair. "Yes, Lieutenant Obvious, I realize that. But I don't have to like it. Are you having any luck?"

"Not really," Bailey admitted, as she half-heartedly scrolled down the page of job offerings.

"Wait a minute, Bales," Emma said as she took control of the mouse on her sister's computer. She pointed to the computer screen and said, "What about that one?"

Bailey looked where her sister pointed and said, "That wasn't there before." She then began reading the job listing aloud. "Associate Pastor wanted. Do you enjoy the slower pace of small-town life? Do you feel more comfortable in a small neighborhood church where you can get to know all your parishioners on a first-name basis? If so, maybe Hope is the place for you. The Associate

Pastor position is waiting to be filled with the right person who can eventually step into the Senior Pastor role. Contact Pastor Travis Harmon by phone or email as listed below."

The two sisters looked at each other and smiled.

"What better place to start your career as a pastor than in a place called Hope," Emma said with determination. "I can hear it calling for you, Bales. I think you need to apply!"

"I don't know, Emma," Bailey said with hesitation. "I would love to get out of the city. But what about you? I wouldn't want to leave my little sister behind with the nerdy twins."

They both laughed at their inside joke, knowing full well they wouldn't trade their brothers for anything.

Emma flexed her muscles and made a determined face. "Come on, Bales. You were in the Army. The boys are no match for the likes of us. You know you want to. Just do it."

"Well, maybe," Bailey replied, quickly warming to the idea. "But…"

Knowing what her sister was about to say, Emma cut her off with a conspiratorial grin. "Don't worry, Bales. You should know by now I'm not that easy to get rid of."

Then, with great fanfare, Emma launched into song. "I will follow you. Follow you wherever you may go!"

"Okay, okay," Bailey said, laughing. "I'll apply for the job, but that doesn't mean I'll get it. Even if I do, that doesn't solve your problem. You know the job market will be a lot better for you in the city."

"Not to worry, Bales," Emma replied with confidence. "It's a God thing. That job offer popped up right when you needed it. You'll apply, then you'll get the job. Then we move to Hope – what a great name for a town – and I'll find a job there." She snapped her fingers as if that solved everything. "Piece of cake!"

Bailey just shook her head. "What would I ever do without

you, Em?"

"You would be hopelessly lost and helpless. Obviously." Emma tapped the computer screen twice. "Time's wasting, Bales. Your job awaits."

Nodding her head, Bailey began typing. "You're right. I have a very good feeling about this job listing. And, for some reason, Hope sounds vaguely familiar. I have no idea why. But something about it rings a bell in the back of my mind."

"Type, Bales," Emma said with a laugh. "I'm going to start packing!"

* * *

A week later, Bailey and Emma were driving across the state to the little town of Hope. Bailey's application for the associate pastor position had been accepted, and she breezed through a phone interview with Pastor Harmon. This morning would be the real test – an in-person interview with the pastor and head elder. Having arrived in town two hours before the scheduled interview, the sisters took some time to drive around Hope.

"What a cute little town," Emma said as she drove through the downtown area.

Bailey nodded her head in agreement. "I love all the old trees scattered through town. And didn't you just want to escape into that park back there? What a great place to have concerts!"

"Oh, look, Bales," Emma said with excitement as she pointed to a sign along the road. "They apparently have a minor league baseball team! Other than family, going to Mariners games is about the only thing I'd miss about Seattle. But I could definitely camp out at a ballpark and watch AAA baseball."

Bailey laughed at her sister's excitement. "Aren't you getting a little ahead of yourself, Em? You're already setting up camp outside their ballpark when I haven't even had the interview yet."

"Minor details, Bales," Emma said confidently. "You're going to ace the interview. Should we drive by the church, so you know where it is before your interview?"

"That's probably a good idea," Bailey replied, checking her phone for the address. "What are you going to do while I'm in the interview?"

"I figured when you're ready to head to the church, I could just hang out in that little coffee shop I saw back there. That way you can take the car and not have to worry about me."

Once they had found the church, Emma parked the car along the curb, then turned off the engine and reached for her phone.

"This will work out great, Bales," Emma said as she looked at her phone. "That little coffee shop is only a block away."

"That's perfect," Bailey agreed. "My interview is in twenty minutes. Let's go ahead and drive over to the coffee shop to drop you off, then I'll come straight back here to the church."

Emma pulled into the parking lot of the coffee shop, then switched places with her sister. Before Bailey got behind the wheel, Emma pulled her into a hug.

"Good luck, Bales," Emma said sincerely. "You're going to do great! I'll be waiting right here when you're done."

"Thanks, Em," Bailey said as she let out the breath she didn't realize she was holding. "Here I go. See you soon!"

Chapter Four

Bailey parked in front of Hope Community Church and smiled as she took in the church and the neatly manicured grounds. This was a very welcoming church, in stark contrast to so many of the churches back home. After sending up a brief prayer regarding her interview, Bailey got out of the car and walked confidently up to the main doors of the church. She wasn't sure exactly where to go, but as she entered the lobby, she saw two men talking near the doors to the sanctuary.

Approaching the men, she asked, "Excuse me, but do you know where I can find Pastor Harmon?"

Travis reached out to shake her hand as he replied, "I'm Pastor Harmon. You must be Bailey Campbell?"

Bailey smiled in relief as she said, "Yes, I am. It's nice to meet you."

Travis glanced at his watch and said with a smile, "Ten minutes early for your interview. You get bonus points."

Already liking this friendly man, Bailey simply smiled.

"Bailey," Travis said by way of introduction, "this is Dave Marshall, the head elder at Hope Community Church."

Dave shook her hand and replied, "It's very nice to meet you, Bailey."

"Dave has been the head elder here longer than I've been the pastor," Travis explained. "He's kind of a permanent fixture at the church. That's one of the reasons I asked him to sit in on your interview. I hope you don't mind."

"Not at all," Bailey replied with more confidence than she felt.

"I'll try not to be too intimidating," Dave said with a chuckle.

"Why don't we go back to my office and get comfortable," Travis said, leading the way. "Would you like a cup of coffee or some water, Bailey?"

"No thank you. I'm fine," Bailey said, following the men through the sanctuary.

Ushering her into the office ahead of them, Travis and Dave followed. Indicating a comfortable chair in front of a large desk, Travis said, "Why don't you have a seat and get comfortable, Bailey? Dave, go ahead and pull up that other chair and join us."

Travis walked around the desk and sat in his chair while everyone settled in. He picked up a piece of paper and scanned it quickly before looking up.

"I shared your resumé with Dave," Travis began. "He was as impressed as I was. You appear to have been a very busy lady the past few years. Top of your class in high school, top of your class in college, then off to the Army and back to college. It seems to me that you're either very driven or you simply know what you want and get busy making it happen. Do you think some of that drive may be from the fast pace of city life?"

"Actually," Bailey replied with a smile, "it may be despite living in the city. Or maybe being in a hurry to escape city life."

"So, tell me, Bailey," Travis began, nodding his head with satisfaction, "what made you want to join the Army, and how did you decide to become a pastor?"

"Well," Bailey said with a small chuckle, "the second was

because of the first. When I was in college to get my Bachelor of Social Work degree, I joined the ROTC."

Dave chuckled in the chair next to her. "Let me guess. You joined ROTC because a friend joined."

Bailey smiled before replying. "You're not far off. I joined because of a dare. College kids do so many silly things on a dare. But this one turned out in my favor. I've always been a person who needs to stay busy, and I wanted something in college that would be a diversion from all the studying and tests. But it needed to be something that wouldn't be a waste of my time. By joining the ROTC, I could enter the Army after college and go in as an officer, a Second Lieutenant."

"You said serving in the Army led to your desire to be a pastor," Travis said. "Tell me how that came about."

"When I enlisted," Bailey began, "I was assigned to the chaplain's office. The chaplain and I hit it off immediately and worked very well together. Before long, he suggested I take the exam for Chaplain Assistant since I was already performing many of those duties anyway. After becoming the CA, I was fortunate enough to be able to spend my entire stint in the same office. I enjoyed my time in the chaplain's office and began to see myself going into pastoring as a career. Since I already had a Bachelor's in Social Work, I decided to return to college after the Army to get my Master's in Divinity. So, here I am!"

Dave and Travis smiled and nodded at this interesting young lady, while the interview continued for another twenty minutes.

After the interview concluded, Travis asked, "Are you heading back to Seattle today, Bailey?"

"Actually," she began in explanation, "my sister and I had decided to spend the night and head back tomorrow afternoon."

"Your sister?" Travis asked.

"Yes, my little sister and I drove over together. She's hanging out over at that little coffee shop down the block."

"Where are you staying tonight?" Dave asked.

"We have a reservation at the Hope Inn," Bailey replied. "We drove by it on our way into town. It looks really cute."

"That would have been my suggestion," Travis nodded in agreement. "If you don't have other plans, my wife and I would love to have you and your sister join us for dinner at our house tonight."

"That would be great!" Bailey replied. "But are you sure? You didn't know my sister would be here. Your wife might not be prepared for company."

Dave laughed before Travis had a chance to reply. "Meghan is always prepared for company. Their house is known for its 'open door' policy."

Travis handed Bailey his business card as they walked toward the door. "I wrote our address on the back. It's just a little ways out of town, and pretty easy to find. Why don't you and your sister plan to stop by around five o'clock? That will give us some time to visit before dinner."

They walked out the door just as a pickup parked next to Bailey's car, and a tall young man climbed out and started toward the door to the church.

Bailey gaped at the man in recognition. "Aiden?" she asked in surprise.

Aiden stopped in his tracks to stare at the young woman in disbelief, "Looie?"

"Oh my," Bailey said softly as Aiden approached her.

Aiden wrapped her in a friendly hug before stepping back, still holding one of her hands. "You look great, Looie. What are the odds of running into you here in Hope?"

Bailey simply shook her head and replied, "I knew when I applied for the job that something sounded familiar about Hope. I just couldn't think what it would be."

"Uh," Travis began with a smile, "Looie? I'm going to need a little explanation here. How is Looie a nickname for Bailey?"

Aiden had finally released Bailey's hand and they both smiled.

"Looie is a very common nickname in the Army for a lieutenant," Aiden explained. "Lieutenant Campbell was the Chaplain Assistant for our unit."

"And you talking about your hometown with such fondness is why the name of the town sounded familiar to me when I saw the job listing," Bailey realized.

"It sounds like the two of you may have some catching up to do," Travis said. "Aiden, Bailey and her sister are staying in town tonight and will be coming over to the house for dinner. Why don't you plan to join us?"

Suddenly, Bailey slapped her forehead. "Emma! I completely forgot about my sister! She's still waiting for me at the coffee shop. If you'll excuse me, I need to go before she sends out a search party!"

Bailey hurried to her car, leaving the three men smiling. This was shaping up to be a very interesting day.

* * *

After the shock of running into Bailey earlier in the day, Aiden had completely forgotten that he had stopped by the church to talk to his uncle about the construction project. When he called Travis after lunch, he was told to come over to the house before the girls arrived and they would have time to talk then. But, for the life of him, Aiden had no clue what he had wanted to discuss.

Looie is here, Aiden thought to himself as he sat in his pickup before heading to his aunt and uncle's house. *She's right here in*

Hope. And she applied for a job here. That means she might be moving here. To Hope. What are the odds? I haven't seen her in two years. She seemed happy to see me… at least I think she did. Wow. If she moves to Hope, I've got to stop thinking of her as Looie. She's no longer Lt. Campbell. She's Bailey Campbell. Bailey. Right here in Hope.

* * *

Aiden had joined his aunt and uncle in their comfortable living room as soon as he arrived. This house had always been his second home, and he didn't think that would ever change. He loved everything about this house and kept the details in his mind whenever he and Matt discussed building houses. They were incorporating many of his aunt's designs into the house they were building for JC and Amy. After talking over some of his ideas with his aunt and uncle, they were now just relaxing and visiting before Bailey and her sister arrived.

"Do you mind if I ask you something, Aiden?" Travis asked during a brief lull in the conversation.

"Not at all," Aiden replied. "You know you can ask me anything."

"You were obviously surprised to see Bailey this morning. But you both seemed happy to see each other. Did you work closely together in the Army?"

"We never really worked together," Aiden replied with a smile. "But she was very involved in all the church services and provided counseling to several of the guys in my unit. One of the guys she was counseling was my best buddy. So, Loo- er, I mean Bailey, and I ran into each other a lot. We became pretty good friends."

"Did you ever date?" Travis asked. "I don't know a lot about how the Army works. Maybe you weren't even allowed to date under those circumstances."

"There was nothing in the regulations that would have prevented us from dating," Aiden replied. "We were very good friends, and we did go out for lunch together occasionally. I don't know if I'd call it dating. We had a lot of respect for each other, and she was easy to talk to. She was fascinated by my hometown and talked a lot about where she grew up. She missed the little town she grew up in near the Canadian border. She was raised on a dairy farm and hated when they moved to the Seattle area."

"Why did she move to Seattle if she loved living in the small town?" Travis asked.

"Her dad apparently developed some software for the dairy industry and eventually moved the family to Seattle when he went to work for Microsoft as a developer. Looie and her sister never liked living in the city, so I'm not surprised she's looking for a job away from that rat race."

"Thanks, Aiden," Travis said. "That helps me a lot."

"What do you mean, Uncle Travis?"

"Bailey's resumé and her qualifications are impeccable," Travis began. "Dave and I were both impressed with her interview. My only real concern was how she might adapt to living in Hope after coming from the Seattle area. She did make a comment about maybe being in a hurry to escape city life."

"From what I understand," Aiden added, "she never liked the big city and hoped to someday settle down far away from the city."

Travis nodded in understanding just as the doorbell rang. "That must be our guests now," he said as his wife walked in from the kitchen.

Travis answered the door, while Meghan and Aiden stood back so their guests could enter the house.

"Hi Bailey," Travis greeted with a smile. "Please come in."

Turning to his wife, Travis said, "This is my wife, Meghan. And you already know Aiden."

With a smile on her face, Bailey handed a small potted plant to Meghan. "It's nice to meet you, Meghan. Emma and I wanted you to have this. We so appreciate you having us for dinner on such short notice. And I'd like everyone to meet my sister, Emma Campbell."

Aiden grinned as he looked from Bailey to Emma. "You two look like you come from different families."

"We get that a lot," Emma laughed. "I look like Mom's side of the family. Bailey and the twins look like Dad's side."

"Twins?" Meghan asked with curiosity. "Our daughter has nine-year-old twins, Aaron and Sophie."

"I just love twins," Emma said. "I hope I can have twins someday. We have twin brothers who are twenty-four. Wyatt and Spencer. They're goofy computer geeks, but we love them anyway."

Everyone laughed as they walked into the living room.

"Have a seat and get comfortable," Meghan said. "Aiden, would you help me bring refreshments in from the kitchen?"

"Sure, Aunt Meghan," Aiden replied.

Returning moments later, Aiden and Meghan set out a tray of cookies and a large pitcher of iced tea.

"Go ahead and help yourselves, everyone," Meghan said. "I hope you ladies like pot roast. Dinner will be ready in about 45 minutes."

Bailey and Emma looked at each other and smiled. "We love pot roast!" Emma answered. "Mom used to get so tired of us requesting it for dinner."

"Please tell me, Aunt Meghan," Aiden said hopefully, "are those your incredible homemade biscuits I smell? Nothing goes better with your pot roast than your homemade biscuits with honey."

Meghan simply smiled, knowing that answered her nephew's question.

"Travis told me a little about you, Bailey," Meghan said. "Emma, why don't you tell us a little bit about yourself so we can get to know you?"

"Well, let's see," Emma began. "I'm the youngest in the family, at twenty-one. I just graduated from Northwest Christian with my Bachelor of Business Administration degree. So, like Bailey, I'm out there looking for a job too. Also, like Bailey, I don't really care for city life. My brothers can keep Seattle. I'll go wherever God decides to send me and hope it's not the big city."

"So, Emma," Travis began, "do I understand correctly that you have a degree in business administration, and you are also looking for a job right now?"

"That's right," Emma confirmed. "There are a lot of job opportunities in the Seattle area, and the pay is great. But I really don't want to continue living in the city. Money isn't everything. I'd rather live someplace I enjoy, instead of existing in a place I don't like and spend my life chasing the all-mighty dollar."

Travis and Meghan looked at each other and smiled.

"Would it be possible for you ladies to stay in town for a couple days, instead of going home tomorrow?" Travis asked.

Bailey and Emma looked at each other and shrugged. "Sure," Bailey replied. "I don't see why not. Do you mind if I ask why?"

"I'd like to discuss your interview with Dave one more time," Travis replied. "I want to be able to give you an answer before you leave town."

Travis then turned to Emma. "And, Emma, I would like to have you meet our daughter Kaci. She has been running the business end of JC's Hope, the youth center our son owns. But now she's also beginning to take on a larger role in the family construction business as some of us old folks start looking toward retirement. I know she wants to step back from the center, and they are planning to look for someone with a business degree to take over her work there. That way she can focus on the construction company."

Emma looked at Bailey with excitement.

"Now," Travis cautioned, "I obviously can't make any promises, and I haven't discussed this with Kaci, but I'd like you to at least meet her."

Emma looked at Bailey and nodded. "We can definitely stay for a couple more days."

Bailey looked across the room and met Aiden's eyes. "This has certainly turned into an interesting day."

* * *

The past few days had been a whirlwind for Bailey and Emma. Travis offered Bailey the Associate Pastor position, and Bailey accepted. Emma met with Kaci, followed by a meeting with her brother JC, the owner of JC's Hope, and his wife Amy. After a tour of the youth center, Emma was offered the newly created position of Business Manager. By the time the sisters had returned to Seattle, they realized their lives were about to change dramatically.

As they were packing their belongings for the move to Hope, Bailey looked at her younger sister. "Emma, do you believe this? We couldn't have asked for a better change. I'm still a little stunned."

Emma smiled at her older sister and said, "Oh, ye, of little faith. Remember what I said at the beginning? You would apply for the pastor job, you would get the job, we would move to Hope, and I would find a job there. Piece of cake. Remember?"

"Ah, but you were wrong, little sis."

"Says Bales as she continues packing," Emma replied with a grin.

"But you *were* wrong. You got a job in Hope before we even moved there!"

Emma laughed as she shook her head. "I guess you've got me there!"

They both plopped down on the sofa in exhaustion, their packing nearly complete. "The icing on the cake," Bailey began, "was when Meghan and Travis told us we could move into their house while we took time to settle in. They even said we could stay there as long as we wanted to. Even with their youngest daughter, Ryleigh, away at school, that still leaves them with two empty bedrooms in their house. Here we are, complete strangers, and they just open their home to us. They're amazing."

"They truly are," Emma agreed. "I can't believe it. We're moving to a place called Hope."

Chapter Five

Matt and Aiden had been working on the new house whenever they had some spare time. With both of them working full-time at Byers Construction, the house-building project was going slower than either of them wanted. But it was satisfying to see the progress. With the help of Todd and Travis, as well as some of the kids in the apprentice program at the high school, the framing had been completed and a good share of the plywood had been installed on the outer walls. They hoped to make a lot of headway over the weekend when they could put in a full day's work.

Aiden was unloading some tools from the back of his pickup when Matt pulled in behind him with his dad in the passenger seat. Matt immediately started helping Aiden with the tools and equipment. As he glanced over to see where his dad was, he saw him leaning against the truck lighting a cigarette.

"Dad," Matt said, "why don't you help us get this equipment unloaded so we're ready to get started as soon as Travis and Todd get here?"

John grumbled under his breath but walked toward the pickup, still fiddling with his cigarette.

Within a few minutes, a Byers Construction pickup pulled onto the lot, followed by Travis in his truck. Both men parked their trucks on the side of the house and began unloading scaffolding. Aiden and Matt jumped in to help get the scaffolding assembled and set in place.

"John," Travis began, "would you grab the rest of the tools from the back of my truck while the boys set up the scaffolding? It would be a big help."

John started toward the truck and began unloading tools, one at a time. Matt glanced over at his dad and shook his head in frustration.

"I'm not sure Dad is being much help," Matt said quietly to Aiden. "It's almost like he wants us to fire him."

"Remember, Matt," Aiden said, "he hasn't worked in a very long time. It's probably going to take some time for him to get the hang of things."

"I suppose," Matt reluctantly agreed. "But you would think he could make more of an effort. He's always more interested in taking smoke breaks than doing any real work."

Aiden patted Matt on the back and said, "Give him time. I wouldn't be surprised if he's smoking more than before to help compensate for giving up the alcohol. Addictions are a terrible thing, Matt."

"I know," Matt agreed. "I guess I just get frustrated because I want to see more progress on the house."

Aiden smiled in understanding. "We'll get it done, Matt. Don't rush it. All in good time."

* * *

Once work began, things progressed rapidly throughout the morning. It was satisfying for everyone involved to see the outer walls nearing completion. Before long, it became obvious they would be able to start installing a few of the smaller windows by the end of the day.

Todd let out a shrill whistle to get everyone's attention. "Why don't we take a little break? Meghan brought over some pizza and soda for lunch. Thanks, sis."

"No problem," Meghan replied, walking toward the front of the house with pizza boxes. "Matt, would you grab the sodas for me, please? We'll put everything inside the living room area so you can spread out a little to eat."

Before long, the guys were sitting on the floor along the walls inside the house, enjoying lunch. John seemed to make a point to separate himself from the group. He sat off to the side, leaning against an opposite wall, even though everyone had asked him to join them. Matt glanced over at his dad, who had a lit cigarette in one hand and a slice of pizza in the other. He could tell his dad had been putting his cigarettes out by crushing them into the plywood subfloor. Matt made a mental note that he would need to sweep up ashes and cigarette butts once again and remind his dad not to smoke in the house.

Meghan began gathering the empty pizza boxes and other trash and filled a garbage bag to take outside to the dumpster.

"Well, Aiden," Meghan said, "it looks like you guys are about finished with the outside plywood."

"Almost," Aiden replied, standing beside Matt. "We have one more small section to finish on the back side of the house, then we can move on from there."

"Todd thinks we'll be able to start installing some of the windows this afternoon," Matt added.

"That's great!" Meghan said. "Have Josh and Amy stopped by lately to see the progress?"

"They came over the other night, just as we were finishing up," Aiden said.

"Yeah," Matt added with a smile. "You can tell they're really excited about the house. Their apartment is great for a couple people. But you can tell they'll be happy to have more room once the baby arrives. I hope we're able to finish the house before then."

Todd walked up behind Matt and put his arm around his shoulder. "You worry too much, Matt," Todd said with a grin. "We'll get the house finished, and it will be great. The kids will be able to get along in the apartment for a little while after the baby arrives if they need to. We're making good progress on the house, so don't worry quite so much."

"You're right, Todd," Matt agreed with a chuckle. "I'm just so excited to see the finished house."

"Well, then," Todd said as he gently nudged Matt toward the back of the house, "let's get that little piece of plywood up so we can install some of those windows."

By the time the small crew called it quits for the day, they had all the bedroom windows installed, as well as the kitchen windows. Todd and Travis had just headed out a few minutes earlier, while Aiden and Matt finished gathering the last of the tools. Travis had offered to take John home, so Matt was able to linger at the house for a while.

Aiden walked up to Matt and put his arm around his shoulder. "It's looking good, isn't it, Matt?"

"It sure is," Matt agreed with a smile. "It's amazing how much more it looks like a house once all the outside sheeting is on and some of the windows are installed."

"This is a good thing we're doing, Matt," Aiden said as they stared at the front of the house. "And I don't just mean building this house for JC and Amy. I mean you and I working together, building houses. It's going to be great. And I can't think of anyone I would rather be doing this with than you. You're like a brother to me, Matt. I'm so glad we're building our dreams together."

Matt turned and looked at Aiden. "Do you mean that, Aiden?"

Aiden simply nodded.

"Being part of your family for the past few years has been the best time of my life," Matt said sincerely. "You have no idea how much it means to me to be considered just another member of the family. It's nice to be able to have dreams. I don't know that I would have had that without you guys. Thank you."

"Why don't you head home and get some rest," Aiden suggested. "You've put in a long day. I'll see you in the morning."

"Yeah, we'll make a short day of it tomorrow. It sounds like it will just be you, me, Todd, and Dad. Travis said he had some things to take care of at the church in the morning."

As the young men started toward their trucks, Aiden said, "Dad told you about the barbecue tomorrow afternoon, right? We're supposed to be at Uncle Travis and Aunt Meghan's by about two o'clock."

"Yeah," Matt confirmed. "He said Mike Slater will be there too. It'll be great to see him. I haven't seen him in a while."

Matt and Aiden took another look at the house and smiled before climbing into their trucks and driving home.

* * *

Todd and Travis had strongly suggested the younger men not push themselves too hard on the house. Matt and Aiden had been putting in some long days working on a commercial building project for Byers Construction, then were burning daylight trying to get more done on the house project. The young men had reluctantly agreed to only work a few hours on the house this morning, then take the afternoon off to join the family for a barbecue at Travis and Meghan's.

By the time they called it quits for the day, they had drilled most of the holes in wall studs to run electrical wire at one end of the house and had installed several more windows. Todd had insisted they wait to install the larger windows in the living and dining rooms until they had more people available to help.

After gathering tools and loading them into the pickups, the men lingered in front of the house, pleased with their progress.

"John," Todd said, "are you sure you don't want to join us for the barbecue this afternoon? You and your wife are both welcome."

"No," John replied as he lit another cigarette. "That's okay. I got things to do at home."

"Okay," Todd nodded. "Matt, why don't you run your dad home then. I'll see you at the house in a bit. We all have time to get cleaned up before heading over to Meghan's."

* * *

When Meghan and Travis put on a family barbecue, it always included any of the family who were in town. They made a point to invite Mike Slater, who had become as much a part of the family as anyone else. Mike joined their family when he became the benefactor and one of the driving forces behind JC's Hope. He had also become a surrogate father figure to Matt's sister Amy and insisted on handling a lot of the wedding expenses when she and JC got married.

Mike had no children of his own. His wife had passed away early in their marriage, and he simply had no desire to remarry. He happily took on the role of "Mr. Mike" to Travis and Meghan's twin grandkids and became a friend and father figure to many of the kids who frequented the youth center.

With another successful barbecue behind them, the older

adults were relaxing on the back deck while Aiden and Matt played catch in the backyard. Although Amy had told Josh to 'go have fun with the guys,' he chose to stay on the deck with his pregnant wife and visit with the family. The twins, Aaron and Sophie, spent most of their time either climbing around on the Bobcat or convincing Mr. Mike to play catch with them.

"Honey," Meghan said to Travis, "you turned off the grill, didn't you?"

"Yes, dear," Travis replied with a smile.

"Okay," she replied. "I thought I smelled smoke. It's probably just the lingering smells from cooking."

Todd glanced over at the grill, which appeared to be cold. "I think you're right, sis. I smell smoke now too."

Some of the adults began looking around, trying to figure out the source of the smell.

Suddenly Matt yelled from the yard as he pointed to the property next door. "Hey, there's smoke coming from next door!"

Before anyone had time to move, flames began shooting over the tops of the trees along the edge of the property.

"Meghan, call 911!" Travis yelled as he started running to his pickup. "Come on, guys! Hop in a truck and let's go!"

The sound of squealing tires, mixed with sirens in the distance, filled the air as the guys hurried next door.

Amy looked at Meghan and Kaci as horror filled her face. "Oh, God. The house…"

Men piled out of pickups just as the fire trucks pulled onto the property and firemen jumped into action. One end of the house under construction was fully engulfed in flames.

Matt started running toward the house and Todd grabbed him by the arm.

"No, Matt," Todd said as he pulled the young man back. "Let the firemen do their job. There's nothing you can do right now."

Aiden walked over to Matt and the two young men put their arms around each other's shoulder. Todd, Travis, JC, Kaci's husband Jason, and Mike looked on in disbelief.

It didn't take long for the firemen to knock down the flames and extinguish the fire. It appeared the end of the house where the bedrooms were located was completely destroyed. The windows that had just been installed had been blown out from the heat, and glass littered the ground.

As the firemen finished ensuring the fire was completely doused, one of the firefighters walked up to the battalion chief. After a brief discussion, which included the chief following the fireman into the house, both men exited the structure and the chief walked toward the men looking on.

"Todd, Travis," the chief said in greeting as they shook hands.

"Doug," both men greeted their friend.

"Do you know what happened, Doug?" Travis asked as the younger men huddled around to hear.

Doug shook his head before replying. "I've been on enough construction sites worked by you guys that this surprised me. Preliminary evidence seems to indicate a cigarette ignited a pile of sawdust. I know none of you guys smoke, so that was a surprise."

"Dad," Matt said quietly, his heart sinking in his chest.

Todd reached out for Matt, but the young man pulled away and walked toward the destroyed end of the house.

"I'll go talk to him, Dad," Aiden said.

"No, son," Todd replied. "Let him be. He needs to be alone right now."

"The fire did a lot of damage," JC said, still in disbelief.

Mike patted him on the back and said, "The damage can be repaired, JC."

Travis looked toward the house to the young man sitting in the open doorway at the front of the house, his head on his knees, having just watched his dreams go up in smoke. "Some of the damage won't be very easy to repair."

Chapter Six

Aiden stood beside his dad and uncle as they took in the scene before them. The damage to one end of the house was extensive, and a lot of work needed to be done before construction could resume. But the men had rounded up extra help for the job. Several employees of Byers Construction eagerly volunteered to help tear down and remove the burnt lumber. JC had reported that no less than a dozen teenagers from the center had volunteered to help as well. He and Mike would be arriving with the teens shortly. The only one missing was Matt.

"Well, guys," Todd said, "this isn't going to be easy. Matt should be here any minute with his dad. He told me he wasn't planning to tell his dad about the fire. He was just going to bring him over and let him see for himself. I'm not sure that's the best way to handle it, but I think we need to trust Matt and take our cues from him."

"I agree," Travis replied with a nod. "Matt has a lot to work through. You both do," he added as he put his arm around his nephew's shoulder.

The men turned toward the street when they heard a pickup pull onto the property. They looked at each other in anticipation, planning to stand back and let Matt handle things with his dad.

Matt and his dad just sat in his pickup for several minutes, looking toward the house. Finally, Matt opened the door and climbed out of his truck. His dad didn't move.

"Come on, Dad," Matt said, with a strained look on his face. "We're going for a walk."

John slowly climbed out of his son's pickup and walked toward him.

"What happened?" John asked.

Matt didn't look at his dad. He simply replied, "Follow me."

John followed his son as they walked toward the house. The others followed but stayed a respectable distance behind.

Matt led his dad to the damaged end of the house, stopping occasionally to shake his head in disbelief. At one point, he bent down and picked up a charred piece of two-by-four, turning it over in his hands.

"Do you know what this is, Dad?" he asked, pinning his dad with a hard stare.

"Anyone can see it's a piece of burnt wood," John replied, still seemingly oblivious to the gravity of the situation.

"No, Dad," Matt said, his voice barely containing his anger. "No, Dad. It's much more than a piece of burnt wood."

Matt shook the piece of wood in his dad's direction before adding, "This is what it looks like when someone's dreams go up in smoke. This is the death of a dream, Dad. My dream. Aiden's dream. JC and Amy's dream. You killed it! You! No one else."

Todd, Travis, and Aiden moved in a little closer, in case they were needed.

"Have you ever in your life given thought to someone other than yourself?" Matt continued, his anger rising. "Do you even care about anyone else? I know you sure didn't care about Amy and me when we were growing up. And it's obvious you still don't care about us."

Matt threw the burnt piece of wood as far as he could toss it, then turned back to his dad. "You did this, Dad! You and your cigarettes!"

John looked down at his hand, still holding a lit cigarette. "I did this, son?"

"Yes, Dad," Matt replied a bit more calmly. "You. You and your cigarettes did this. I have tried to help you, but you don't seem to care. We hired you to help out on the house to give you a chance to earn some money and maybe regain your self-esteem. I tried, Dad. I really tried."

Anger and sadness forced tears from Matt's eyes. He turned away from his dad and said quietly. "I tried, Dad. I can't do this anymore. I won't allow you to destroy any more of my life, or my dreams. I just can't do this anymore."

John slowly walked up to his son and placed his hand on his back. He turned Matt to face him and held out his pack of cigarettes.

"Here, son," he said, forcing himself to look his son in the eyes. "I'm done. You've turned out to be quite a man. No thanks to me," he scoffed. "I certainly don't deserve you."

Since Matt made no move to take the cigarettes from his dad's hand, John crushed the entire pack in his hands and tossed them on the ground.

"I know there's no way I can undo the damage I've done," John began. "Not the damage to you, or the damage to this house. And I will try to understand if you say you never want to see me again, but I hope that's not the case. I want to help repair the damage to the house if I can. And I hope you'll give me a chance to repair the damage I've done to our relationship. It's a lifetime of damage, and it sure won't be easy. But I want to try. If you'll let me."

Matt gave no indication what he was thinking. He simply

stared back at his dad.

Aiden walked over to Matt and placed his hand on his shoulder. "It's an olive branch, Matt. Take it. We're all here for you and we'll help in any way we can. But take it, Matt."

Aiden then turned and pointed to the house. "That's just a house, Matt." Then he tapped himself on the chest and said, "Our dreams live here," as he pointed to Matt's heart. "No one can take away our dreams unless we let them. Take the olive branch, Matt."

Matt faced his dad and let out a huge sigh as his shoulders sagged. He took another look at the house, then turned back to his family.

"Well, people," Matt began, "it looks like we have a lot of work to do. We might as well get started." Then he reached over and shook his dad's hand.

* * *

With the help of several guys from Byers Construction, as well as teenagers from the youth center, work to tear down and remove burnt lumber continued throughout the morning. Two dump trucks from Byers Construction kept up a steady stream of hauling off debris. Meghan delivered coolers with cold bottled water for the volunteers, and Mike sent word with Meghan that he would be bringing pizza for lunch.

Just before noon, Mike arrived and parked his pickup near the front of the house where Meghan had already set up folding tables and chairs. She had also rigged up a makeshift washing station where the volunteers could wash their hands before lunch. Mike honked the horn on his truck to get everyone's attention.

Once most of the noise stopped, Mike said loudly, "Take a break and come get some pizza. There's pizza, breadsticks, and cold drinks. Help yourselves!"

After washing up, volunteers quickly surrounded the tables loaded with food and filled their plates. Some of the people took advantage of the tables and chairs, while others went back to the house to sit on the floor of the undamaged living room.

Matt, covered in dirt and soot from head to toe, walked up to Mike and thanked him for supplying lunch.

"It's my pleasure, Matt," Mike said as he looked toward the house. "You guys have already made a lot of progress. It's true what they say about many hands making light work."

"Yeah," Matt agreed. "I don't know what we would have done if all these people hadn't offered to help."

Mike patted Matt on the back, both laughing at the cloud of dust it created. "Go get something to eat, son. And rest a little. It's barely noon and you already look completely worn out."

When it looked like everyone had been through the food line, Travis walked up to Todd as he was grabbing a slice of pizza.

"Have you seen John?" Travis asked.

"Last time I saw him," Todd replied, "he was around on the back side of the house breaking up lumber to toss in the dump truck. He's been working every bit as hard as the teenagers. I've got to hand it to him."

"I think I'll go look for him," Travis said. "I want to make sure he gets something to eat."

Travis walked toward the back of the house, with a bottle of cold water in his hand, in search of Matt's dad. He found him bent over a pile of charred wood, breaking it into manageable pieces.

"John," Travis said as he approached, "you need to take a break and get something to eat."

When Matt's dad looked up, his face was covered in dirt, soot, and sweat. He took off his ball cap and wiped his filthy shirt sleeve across his forehead.

Travis opened the bottle of water and handed it to the tired man.

"Sit down, John," Travis said. "You need to take a break."

John took the bottle of water with a nod, then walked over and sat on the ground, leaning against the back of the house.

Travis had been working alongside the others all morning and was as tired as anyone. But he was very much aware of the fact that John wasn't used to putting in long hours of manual labor. Travis sat down next to John and took a long drink from his own water bottle.

"You don't have to work yourself to death to prove something to Matt," Travis said quietly.

John simply looked at him doubtfully but didn't reply.

"I mean it, John," Travis insisted. "Don't kill yourself to prove a point. You still have a family who needs you."

John took a drink of water, then stared off into space.

"I don't know how I can ever make this up to Matt," John said, his voice filled with regret. "I've got to do something to prove to him I have some good in me. That's a tall order. He's never seen anything but disappointment in me. You know, I used to be different. When I was younger, I was a hard worker, just like Matt. Then I got mixed up with alcohol and, as they say, the rest is history."

Travis looked over at the defeated man who had tears forming in his eyes.

"I just want my boy to be proud of me," John said quietly.

"One day at a time, John," Travis said as he touched the man's arm. "Matt will come around before you know it. He was pretty angry at first, and rightfully so. But he's learned a lot about himself in the past few years. He's learned that anger doesn't accomplish anything, he's learned to forgive, and he's learned that he's allowed to have dreams. I'm not sure he believed that before. I think that's why this has been so hard for him. It was the first time he had allowed himself to dream big dreams. And he felt you took that away from him. Give him time, John."

John shook his head before standing. "Matt doesn't deserve the kind of dad I've been to him. But I'm going to do everything I can to change that." With a weak smile, John turned back and asked, "Did you say there was pizza somewhere? I could sure use some."

"Come on," Travis said as he started around the end of the house. "Let's get something to eat before we get back to work."

* * *

By the end of the day, everyone was amazed at the amount of progress that had been made. Most of the burnt portion of the house had been torn down and hauled away. Only a small section remained to be dismantled. Once the last of the debris was hauled off, the only task remaining would be cleanup and some prep work before construction could resume.

After the volunteers left, Travis and Todd took a seat on the tailgate of Todd's truck. Matt, his dad, and Aiden were sitting on the ground near the pickups. They were all too tired to speak. Mike walked over from his truck with an armful of bottled water and handed one to each of the men.

Matt was the first to speak. "Thanks doesn't begin to cover what you all have done today. But thanks is all I've got to give. So, thank you."

"Same goes for me," Aiden added. "Every one of you really stepped up for us, and we certainly appreciate it. Once we regroup, we'll figure out what to do from here."

Mike looked around at the group of exhausted men but focused his attention on Aiden and Matt. "You boys know this is a good thing you've been doing here, right? You thought it would be great to be able to build houses someday, and you wanted the first house to be a gift for JC and Amy. This first house is important. But it hasn't been easy. Take it from me, the first of anything never comes easy. There are always going to be setbacks. There are going to be things that don't work out the way you had hoped. But you learn from all those 'firsts' and keep moving forward.

"You two are remarkable young men, and I have no doubt one day there will be several homes scattered around town that have been built by you. But first, you have to finish this house. So, put your heads together, figure out what supplies you need to resume construction, and get things ordered. Put it on my tab. Whatever you need, make it happen. I am officially investing in your future. Just don't forget to invite me to the open house for JC and Amy's new home."

Matt and Aiden jumped up and walked over to thank Mike. Matt wrapped Mike in a big hug and said quietly, "You won't regret it, Mike. I promise."

Matt then walked back over to his dad, still sitting on the ground. He reached his hand out to help him up.

"Dad," Matt said, with tears forming in his eyes, "I want to thank you for all your work today. You worked as hard as anyone, and you wouldn't stop. Travis had to practically force you to stop long enough to eat a slice of pizza. I know I was hard on you earlier, and I wish I could say I was sorry, but it needed to be said."

John nodded, before saying, "You were right, Matt. It needed to be said. I'm glad you had the guts to call out your old man when he was wrong."

"Yes, that needed to be said," Matt continued. "But this needs to be said too. I'm proud of you, Dad. You did an honest day's work today in an effort to correct your mistake. I can't expect any more than that from anyone."

John pulled his son into a tight hug and sobbed into the shoulder of his dirty shirt.

When he stepped back, Matt looked at him and said with a chuckle, "Before you were just dirty. Now you're wet and dirty!"

And they hugged again.

Chapter Seven

Having temporarily relocated most of their furnishings to a Seattle storage unit before the big move, Bailey pulled her SUV off to the side of the road just before entering the town of Hope. Emma parked her small Honda behind her sister's car, then got out and walked up to Bailey as she climbed out of her SUV.

"Well, Em," Bailey said with a smile as she leaned against her car, "this is it. We're finally here and can begin this new chapter in our lives."

Emma looked at the "Welcome to Hope" sign a few yards in front of them, then snapped a picture of it with her phone.

"I just love that sign," she said. "Welcome to Hope – Where Dreams Come Alive."

Bailey nodded in agreement. "I have such a good feeling about this move, Em. I can easily see us both building our futures here."

Emma glanced at the time on her phone and said, "We should get going. We told Travis and Meghan to expect us about ten-thirty and it's after ten now. I think I remember how to get to their house, but I've got the address plugged into my phone, just in case."

Less than twenty minutes later, the two vehicles pulled into the driveway of their temporary home. Travis, Meghan, and two young men were sitting on the front porch awaiting their arrival.

Travis was the first to meet the ladies in the driveway. "It's good to see you, ladies. How was the drive over the pass?"

"The weather was beautiful," Bailey replied. "We even stopped at the summit to enjoy the scenery. The falls are breathtaking."

Travis turned to the small group behind him, then addressed the ladies. "You both remember Meghan and Aiden from your last visit." Then he chuckled and added, "Well, Bailey apparently knew Aiden already, but I don't think either of you have met Matt."

Matt reached out his hand to introduce himself. "Hi, I'm Matt. You'll be seeing me around a lot. As Travis and Meghan have figured out, I'm kind of hard to get rid of."

Meghan gave Matt a motherly nudge on the shoulder and said, "We wouldn't have it any other way, Matt."

Aiden stepped up to Bailey and said, "Matt and I are going to help unload your cars. Your rooms are upstairs, so don't worry about carrying anything. We'll get it."

Bailey smiled as she looked at Aiden, not really seeing Matt. "Thanks, Aiden. We really appreciate it."

Since they didn't have any furnishings, it wasn't long before all their belongings had been taken to their rooms – the guys had even hung all the clothes in their respective closets. The girls were surprised to see how nice and comfortable their rooms were. Both rooms had a bed, a dresser, and two nightstands, along with a small desk. The roomy closets were a bonus. Meghan had even put a vase with fresh flowers on one of the nightstands in each room. After stowing their suitcases in the closets, the girls joined the others downstairs.

"Let's go out onto the deck," Meghan suggested. "I have

some snacks ready, and everyone can relax a bit."

"Matt," Aiden said, "if you grab the tray of cookies, I'll get the iced tea and glasses."

Matt's eyes instantly lit up at the tray of Meghan's homemade chocolate chip cookies.

"On second thought," Aiden said with a chuckle as he picked up the tray of cookies, "I think I'll take these out. Cookies aren't safe with you!"

Putting the refreshments on a table on the deck, Aiden gestured for Bailey to sit in one of the love seats and he sat down beside her.

Bailey looked out over the spacious backyard and remarked, "This is so refreshing after years of living in a small apartment… or Army housing. It's nice to see so much open space."

Emma had settled into one of the other love seats, where Matt wasted no time joining her. "I know what you mean, Bales. I can certainly get used to this life. It sure beats the ant race."

"Ant race?" Matt asked. "Don't you mean rat race?"

With a chuckle, Emma explained, "Bailey and I have always referred to city living as the ant race, because every time we look out our fourth-floor apartment window, it looks like a bunch of ants scurrying around."

"Our *former* fourth-floor apartment," Bailey corrected with a smile.

"Ah," Emma sighed. "That sure has a nice ring to it."

Meghan looked over at the girls, who were both wearing happy smiles. "Since you have the whole afternoon ahead of you to relax, do you think you girls will be up for a welcome dinner with some of the family tonight? I thought we'd have a spaghetti feed and give you a chance to meet some of the rest of the family. But only if you're up to it. If not, we could do it another night."

Emma looked over at her sister. "I'm game if Bailey is."

"It sounds great to me," Bailey agreed. "Let's do it. Is there something Emma and I can do to help?"

Travis laughed before saying, "Meghan and Kaci have spaghetti dinners down to a science – especially for large crowds. They've even trained Amy. When they put on a spaghetti feed, it's like watching a fine-tuned symphony."

Turning to his wife, Travis asked, "How many people are we talking about? We don't want to chase the girls off their first day in town."

"I think they'll be fine," Meghan said. "They've already met most of them anyway. But let's see…" Counting on her fingers, she continued, "There's you and me, Kaci, Jason and the twins, Josh and Amy, Todd and Nicole, Aiden and Matt, then, of course, Mike. I guess that makes about fifteen counting Bailey and Emma. Is that too many for you girls?"

"No, that's just fine," Bailey assured them.

"The more the merrier," Emma added.

"It's settled, then," Meghan said with a smile. "I'll go make some quick phone calls to confirm with everyone. You girls just make yourselves at home. If you get tired of people and need some space, feel free to escape into your rooms or the living room or family room. This is your home now, so we want you to feel comfortable."

"Actually," Bailey said, "after spending the morning in the car, I could use a little walk to stretch my legs."

"Hey, Matt," Aiden said eagerly, "why don't we take the girls next door to see the house?"

Matt jumped up, quickly agreeing. "That's a great idea!"

He reached his hand out to help Emma up, then grabbed a fist full of cookies from the tray.

When Emma looked at him with a grin, he explained with a shrug, "Snacks for the trip."

"Trip?" she asked. "I thought you said it was just next door."

Matt and Emma started down the stairs off the deck. "It is. But this is a fair-sized lot, and the house next door sits on a five-acre lot. So, we might get hungry."

Travis laughed as Aiden simply shook his head then reached his hand out to help Bailey up.

"We won't be gone long, Uncle Travis," Aiden said.

"No need to hurry," Travis reassured them. "I'm just going to see if Meghan needs any help, then I'll be in the study working on my sermon."

* * *

The four young adults walked partway down the driveway, then cut across the yard to get to the property next door. During the short walk, Aiden and Bailey chatted like old friends, and Matt and Emma got to know each other a bit.

Once they got to the house, Emma walked ahead of the others and said, "Wow, what happened? It looks like there was a fire."

Matt walked up beside her and said, "It's kind of a long story. Let's take the grand tour, and Aiden and I will tell you all about it."

"Is it safe to go inside?" Emma asked.

"Oh, yeah," Aiden replied. "It's perfectly safe."

After walking around the outside of the house to get a feel for its size, they stopped at the opening where the front door would go. Aiden stepped up into the house, then reached for Bailey's hand to help her up.

"Watch your step," he cautioned. "Obviously there will eventually be a deck and steps to get into the house."

Matt helped Emma up and through the door opening as well and she immediately began exploring.

"This is pretty cool," she said, as she checked out the different rooms. "I've never been inside a house that's under construction. It's kind of fun seeing the open walls and stuff."

The guys stayed back and allowed the girls to explore the house. Once they returned to the living room area, Bailey plopped down in the middle of the floor and patted the floor next to her. The four young adults sat in a circle in the middle of the living room.

"So, tell us about this house," Bailey said.

Aiden and Matt looked at each other and smiled.

"Well," Aiden began, "a while back, Matt mentioned that someday he'd like to try building houses on the side. You see, Aunt Meghan and Uncle Travis are both expert carpenters. Aunt Meghan was actually building their current house next door when they met. Uncle Travis has built several custom homes. Anyway, Matt thought it would be cool to try building houses. So, he and I talked about doing it together. Our family supported the idea, so we started planning for the first one, which is going to be a gift to JC and Amy."

"Wow," Bailey said, clearly impressed.

Matt piped in, "So, Aiden and I have been building this house in our spare time. Todd and Travis have helped a lot. We couldn't have done it without them."

"Amen!" Aiden quickly agreed.

"We hired my dad to help out with some of the basic work," Matt continued. "He hasn't worked in a long time, and he just went through rehab a couple years ago. We were hoping to give him a chance to earn some money and ease back into the working world. He was kind of having a tough time of it and wasn't putting a whole lot of effort into the work. Just kind of going through the motions, you know? Anyway, Dad's a smoker, and one day he apparently left a cigarette butt in one of the bedrooms where we had been working. The cigarette wasn't completely out and ended up catching a pile of sawdust on fire. It destroyed the end of the house where the bedrooms were."

Emma reached over and touched Matt's arm. "I'm so sorry, Matt. That had to be really hard for you, putting all that work into the house and then having that happen."

Matt and Aiden both nodded somberly.

"Yeah," Aiden continued. "It was tough for everyone. Even Matt's dad when he saw the damage and realized he had caused it. But our community is amazing. The entire family stepped up to help out. Some of the guys from the family construction company came over, and so did a bunch of teens from JC's youth center. Everyone pitched in to help. Before long, all the burnt portions had been dismantled and hauled off. Now we're getting ready to resume construction."

Emma stood and began walking around the inside of the house again. "It's pretty exciting that you're building this house for JC and Amy. Do they know it's for them, or will it be a surprise? Since I'll be working with them, I wouldn't want to accidentally ruin a surprise."

Matt smiled as he said, "They know the house will be for them. They're super excited about it, especially since they have a baby on the way. It will be nice for them to get out of their apartment and into a house, hopefully before the baby arrives. I think we were pretty much on track before the fire. With that setback, I'm not sure the house will be finished in time."

"Like Dad said, Matt," Aiden said as a reminder, "the house will get finished when it gets finished. They'll be able to make do at the apartment for a while, even with the baby, if they need to."

Emma stood and spun like Maria from *The Sound of Music* in the middle of the large open room. "I think it's exciting! I can't wait to have a house of my own someday."

Matt smiled as Aiden stood and reached for Bailey's hand, helping her up.

"Well, ladies," Aiden began, "shall we head back next door? Unless there's something else you two would like to do?"

Emma smiled at Matt and said, "I wouldn't want to wear out our welcome on our first day here, but I seem to remember passing a little ice cream parlor as we came through town. Is anyone interested in getting some ice cream?"

"I'm always up for the Hope Creamery!" Matt replied quickly.

"Didn't you just have several cookies, Matt?" Aiden asked with a chuckle.

"Hey," Matt replied as he flexed his biceps, "I need to keep my strength up."

The girls laughed as they walked back across the lot toward the cars.

"Let's take my car," Bailey said.

"Sounds good to me," Aiden agreed. "I'll text Aunt Meghan and let her know where we're going. We won't be gone too long."

The four piled into Bailey's SUV and headed out for their first adventure.

* * *

The smell of spaghetti sauce and garlic bread filled the air and happily mingled with the sounds of family. Bailey and Emma had met the rest of the family, except for Ryleigh who was still away at school, finishing up her master's degree. Emma captured the hearts of the twins when she told them how lucky they were to be nine, the last age before hitting double digits.

After everyone had enjoyed another spectacular spaghetti dinner, and pitched in to get all the cleanup done, people scattered around the family room and engaged in lively conversation as they made Bailey and Emma feel like they had been part of the family forever. Emma immediately liked Amy and claimed her as another sister. Mike was anxious to hear all about Bailey's time in the Army, curious to hear how different it was from a woman's perspective. Aiden was happy to see how quickly his family welcomed Bailey and Emma into their lives. And Todd didn't miss how Matt and Emma seemed to be instantly drawn to each other.

Sophie had been begging her Uncle Josh to play some music on the piano in the family room, and he finally agreed, putting a huge smile on her little face. When Bailey mentioned that Emma also played piano, JC smiled and patted the piano bench beside him. Emma joined him and before long the house was filled with music of all types. They played everything from kids' songs to contemporary pop, gospel music, and everything in between.

During a break in the music, Amy looked at Emma and said, "You know, Emma, now that Josh knows you play the piano, don't be surprised if he doesn't usher you down to the music room at the center occasionally. He's always looking for someone to team up with him on the keyboard."

Emma laughed and said, "I wouldn't object to that at all. We never had a piano at the apartment, so I don't get to play very often. The bigger problem would probably be him finding me in the music room when I'm supposed to be doing the bookwork!"

JC just laughed as he said, "That's not a bad problem to have. By the way, Emma, did we ever decide when you plan to start working with Kaci?"

Kaci was in the middle of a friendly wrestling match with her son Aaron over control of a bean bag chair when she heard her name.

"I surrender, Aaron," she said laughing. "You can have the

bean bag. I have to talk business now so that probably wouldn't look good from a bean bag anyway."

Emma chuckled before replying, "I don't know. I think that looks like a pretty comfortable way to conduct business."

Kaci looked at JC and said, "It sounds like you might need to put a bean bag in the office at the center. I could see Emma camped out in a bean bag with a laptop, happy as a clam."

Emma laughed in agreement.

"In answer to your question," Kaci said, "we never really pinned down a date. I was thinking she might want a few days to get settled in here before she starts training.

"What do you think, Emma?" Kaci asked. "My schedule is flexible, so I'll leave it up to you."

"Maybe two or three days to get settled in," Emma replied. "That would give me a chance to drive around town and get the lay of the land and find out where things are."

"I could drive you around and show you the town," Matt suggested hopefully. "I have some time tomorrow if you'd like."

"That'd be great, Matt," Emma replied.

"You know, Bailey," Aiden added, "it would probably be a good idea for you to get familiar with the town as well. If it works for you ladies, and Matt agrees, maybe the four of us could do that sometime tomorrow. Maybe we could even grab lunch while we're out."

"That sounds good to me," Matt agreed. "As long as the sightseeing tour also includes a stop at the Creamery."

"You know, Matt," Emma said with a smile, "you're pretty easy to figure out. Cookies, ice cream, more ice cream."

"Yep," Matt replied with a grin. "I'm not complicated. Just keep me fed."

After additional discussions, it was decided both the girls would take a few days to settle in. At the first of the week, Emma would start training with Kaci to take over the business end of things at the center, and Bailey would begin working with Travis at the church.

Seated next to Aiden on the sofa, Bailey looked around the room swirling with conversation, and knew her heart was happy.

"This," she said quietly to no one in particular. "This is what I want."

Chapter Eight

Bailey and Emma were sitting in the chairs on the front porch, soaking up the morning sunshine when Aiden and Matt pulled into the driveway. The girls could tell by the way the guys were dressed that they had planned to make a day of the outing. Both men were wearing nice Levis. While Matt had opted for a polo shirt, Aiden was wearing a button-up shirt. Both girls were wearing nice jeans, paired with a brightly colored top.

Aiden parked his pickup off to the side of the driveway so he wouldn't be blocking anyone in. "Good morning, ladies," Aiden greeted as they approached the porch. "Are you ready for the grand tour?"

"Hi guys," Bailey and Emma replied simultaneously.

"Emma and I were talking," Bailey began, "I think it would make sense to take my SUV. It has more legroom than Emma's Honda, and definitely more room than your pickup."

"I agree," Aiden said. "But, since you don't know your way around town, would you mind if I drove?"

Bailey smiled as she replied, "I was going to suggest that, but didn't want to put you on the spot."

As the four young adults walked toward Bailey's SUV, Matt turned to Emma. "I didn't realize your hair was so long. It was up in a ponytail yesterday."

"The ponytail was definitely more practical for moving day," Emma said with a smile. "But I usually wear it down."

Matt reached around Emma and opened the car door for her, closing it once she was seated. Aiden opened the front passenger door for Bailey, then went around the car and got into the driver's seat after closing her door.

After adjusting the seat and mirrors, Aiden looked at Matt in the rearview mirror. "Where should we head first, Matt? Any thoughts?"

"Ladies," Matt addressed the girls, "is there anything you're especially interested in seeing?"

"Anywhere except the mall!" Emma replied. "Some place that convinces us we really are out of the city." At the boys' shocked expressions, Emma laughed and continued, "No mall for me, unless I'm going there for something specific. Otherwise, I'd just as soon go to a ballpark, batting cages, or concerts in the park. Hey, do they actually have concerts in that really cool park we saw when we first came to town?"

"Concerts?" Matt asked as if he had missed part of the conversation.

Aiden chuckled and said in explanation, "You lost him at 'batting cages.' Matt was the star shortstop in high school. It sounds like there will be a trip to the batting cages in your future. Not today though. We're not dressed for it."

"Of course not," Emma agreed. "That would definitely be a ponytail day!"

The four laughed as they pulled out of the driveway and headed toward town.

* * *

The next two hours were spent driving around town, with the boys pointing out various places, while the girls worked on getting their bearings. The tour included a brief stop at JC's Hope since Bailey hadn't been there yet. While there, JC and Amy explained how the center came to be and assured her she was welcome to stop by anytime. They also swung by Byers Construction so the girls could see where the guys spent most of their time. And, although it was closed, they drove by the stadium, home to the Hope Angels.

A short time later, Aiden pulled into a shady spot at the park and parked the car. "I assume this is the park you mentioned seeing when you first came to town. There are other parks in town, but this is the largest one, and we do have concerts here."

The four got out of the car and started walking toward the park. "This is the most beautiful park," Bailey said as she took it all in. "I just love all the old trees. It reminds me of a park back home."

"I agree, Bales," Emma said with a smile. "We used to spend hundreds of hours hanging out in that park. I can already tell this is going to be one of my favorite places in town. This, and the ballpark!"

"Ah," Matt said with a smile, "a girl after my own heart."

With a lighthearted wink at Emma, Aiden said, "You'll never get rid of him now!"

Emma smirked. "Well, I've only known him for a couple of days, but he's pretty cute, and he likes baseball. Maybe I won't want to get rid of him."

Matt puffed out his chest and replied with a chuckle, "See, Aiden, the ladies like baseball players."

Bailey playfully bumped Aiden's shoulder and said, "I don't know. Some ladies like Army men."

"In that case, ladies," Aiden said, "why don't you let this

former Army man and former baseball player take you to lunch."

"And ice cream!" Matt added. "You said this tour would include a stop at the Creamery. I'm going to hold you to that!"

Emma laughed as she took Matt by the arm and led him to the car, "Come on, shortstop. Lunch first, then ice cream."

* * *

Over the next few weeks, life began to settle into a new routine for everyone. Bailey was getting her feet wet in her new role as Associate Pastor at Hope Community Church and was enjoying getting to know some of the parishioners. Emma was quickly learning the ropes at JC's Hope, which freed up a lot of time for Kaci to be able to concentrate on the construction company. Amy still spent a fair amount of time at the youth center, so she and Emma were becoming fast friends. On the days when Amy didn't stop by, Emma made a point to call and check on her in case she wasn't feeling well or needed something. Amy certainly wasn't lacking in people who genuinely cared about her and tried to help make her pregnancy comfortable.

Aiden and Matt stayed very busy working at Byers Construction and continued to make progress on the house in their spare time. With help from Travis, Todd, and some of the guys from the construction company, the destroyed part of the house was close to being rebuilt. Matt's dad was at the house working whenever work was being done. He had gotten into a routine with the others, so his contribution was greatly appreciated. He even took an interest in learning new things and was soon working alongside Matt building walls. And somehow, even with everyone's busy lives, Aiden and Matt still managed to find time to spend with Bailey and Emma.

After hearing regular updates about progress at the house, the girls had been wanting to check it out but preferred to go with the guys. Aiden's pickup pulled into his aunt and uncle's driveway just as the girls walked out onto the front porch. Matt climbed out of the passenger seat and walked up to Emma with a smile on his face.

"Hi Emma," he said in greeting. "You look nice. What's with the ponytail?"

Emma chuckled as she replied, "I tried out the rock-climbing wall at the center today. I've been staring at the dang thing for two weeks, trying to get up the nerve to try it."

"That's awesome!" Matt said with excitement. "How'd you do?"

"I got about halfway up," Emma replied. "I could have gone further, but I know JC wants people to have spotters when they're climbing the wall. There wasn't anyone around to spot me, so I didn't want to go any further."

"Next time you want to climb, let me know," Matt offered. "I'd be happy to spot you."

"Thanks," she replied with a smile. "I'll remember that."

While Matt and Emma were visiting, Aiden had joined Bailey on the front porch where they were standing beside each other, leaning against the porch railing, looking over the front lawn.

"I just love this property," Bailey said. "It's beautiful. And it's so quiet and peaceful here."

Aiden nodded. "Aunt Meghan was very particular about what she wanted when she was looking for property to build her house. And they've done a great job with the landscaping. Of course, that was a long time ago, before JC or Ryleigh were born. But I agree. I've always loved this property and the house. It's been my second home my entire life."

"There are so many things about Hope, and this property, that remind me of home," Bailey said wistfully. "Now that I'm finally out of Seattle, I can't imagine ever moving back to another city."

"Then you should plan to stick around Hope," Aiden said with a smile, as he gave Bailey a friendly bump on the shoulder.

"I don't have any plans to leave," Bailey replied. "Not anytime soon. Maybe never."

"I'd be okay with that," Aiden said quietly, taking her hand. "Let's see if they're ready to walk over to check out the house."

Aiden still had Bailey's hand in his as the four walked across the yard to the property next door. Emma ran ahead of Matt as they approached the house.

"This is looking great!" Emma said with excitement as she walked toward the opening of the front door. "Can we go inside, Matt?"

"Sure," Matt replied, coming up behind her. "Here," he said, taking her hand, "let me help you. I don't need you to fall climbing into the house."

Emma laughed as she replied, "Hey, I climbed a rock wall today, remember? I'm pretty sure I can step up into the house. But it will be easier once the deck is built."

Matt stepped up into the house behind her, then gently placed his hand on the small of her back as he guided her off to the side so the others could get into the house.

"Wow!" Emma said in amazement. "You guys have done a lot of work! It looks like this end of the house is almost rebuilt."

"Yeah," Aiden said as he followed them to the end of the house. "The inside is almost back to where it was before the fire. We just need to finish getting the plywood back on the roof. I think we're going to try to roof the entire house next week. Isn't that the plan, Matt?"

"I think so," Matt agreed. "It will be nice to have the roofing on. Then I think we're going to start working on the siding. Won't be long and it will really start taking shape."

Bailey walked up to Aiden and put her hand on his back. "I think it's so great the two of you are building this house together. JC and Amy are going to love it. Did you guys say you were planning to build more houses after this one?"

"That's the hope," Aiden said. "We have to see how this one turns out first. If everything goes well, we plan to start building houses on the side, in our spare time."

"If we do that," Matt added, "it will definitely keep us busy! But the nice thing is that it's something we could call our own. I love working at Byers Construction, and I don't plan to stop doing that. I'm sure Aiden feels the same way. But if we build houses together, that would be ours. Something we did, from start to finish. That would really be cool."

"It'll happen," Emma said confidently as she walked up to the others. "I have no doubt it'll happen. You guys are hard workers. If you say you want to do it, you'll find a way to make it happen."

"Thanks, Emma," Matt said as he casually took her hand. "And for that vote of confidence, you get ice cream. We'll even let Aiden and Bailey join us."

Emma laughed as she led him toward the front door. "Did you really need an excuse for ice cream, Matt? It's probably a good thing you work so hard. You have to work off all those cookies and ice cream!"

"Hey," Matt said with a chuckle, "I told you I wasn't complicated. Just keep me fed."

With that, Emma took off running toward the car. "Last one to the car has to buy the ice cream!"

Matt started running, with Aiden and Bailey close on his heels. "Hey," he said as he stopped suddenly, "why am I running? As long as I get ice cream, I don't care who's buying it!"

Aiden looked back at him. "Good thing you're buying then since you eat the most anyway."

Reaching into the back pocket of his Levis to make sure he had his wallet, Matt jogged over to the car with a smile on his face.

Chapter Nine

Crack! ... Crack! ... Crack! The sound pierced the relatively early morning calm near the high school. Crack! Then laughter.

"Come on, Matt," Emma pleaded. "Quit hogging the machine!"

"Okay, okay," he laughed. "Your turn."

Emma took the baseball bat from him and stepped up to the plate. The pitching machine began hurling baseballs faster than she could swing. She began swinging erratically, missing every pitch because she was laughing so hard.

She held up her hand and stepped back. "No fair," she said. "I'm used to softball, not baseball!"

"Hey," he said with a smile, "you're the one who wanted to hit the batting cages."

Emma scowled at him and said, "Yeah, but I didn't tell you to set the speed at 90 miles per hour!"

Matt laughed and stepped up behind her. "Here, let me help."

He reached around her and repositioned her hands on the bat, then triggered the pitching machine. With Matt's help, Emma hit the first pitch. She turned to look at him, wearing a victory smile. Without thinking, Matt leaned down and gently kissed her, not realizing he still had his arms around her.

Suddenly, he dropped his hands and stepped back. "Sorry, Emma," he apologized as the back of his neck turned slightly red. "I don't know why I did that."

A faint blush crept up Emma's cheeks as she reached over and grabbed the front of his shirt, gently pulling him into another tender kiss.

She looked up into his eyes and said quietly, "Yeah, I don't know why I did that either."

The two stood transfixed for a moment before Matt reached over and shut down the pitching machine.

"Uh," Matt said as he smiled at Emma, "I guess we'd better both get to work. Do you still want to come over to the house tonight to help us put up some more siding? Meghan invited me and Aiden over for dinner before we get started."

Still never breaking eye contact, Emma replied, "Yeah, I'd like that. Sounds like fun."

As they walked toward their vehicles, Emma reached out and took Matt's hand in hers, the earlier tension having quickly evaporated. With a grin, she said, "We'd better get to work, shortstop, before people come looking for us."

When they got to Emma's car, Matt leaned over and gave her a light peck on the cheek. "See you tonight, slugger."

* * *

After another delicious meal with Travis and Meghan, Matt reluctantly pushed his chair away from the table.

"Well, Aiden," Matt began, "if we're going to get some siding on the house tonight, we'd better get started."

"Did you want to come with us, Bailey?" Aiden asked hopefully. "Emma's coming over to help."

Bailey stood and looked at Meghan. "I can stay and help you

with the dishes if you need me to, Meghan."

Meghan chuckled and said, "That's what dishwashers are for Bailey. You girls go ahead and help the guys. Putting up siding always goes faster if you have extra hands."

Turning to Aiden and Matt, Meghan added, "Oh, I almost forgot. Todd said he was planning to stop by to help with siding tonight too. Nicole is working the graveyard shift at the hospital this week, so he claims he's bored."

"Whatever excuse he finds to help," Aiden said with a chuckle. "We'll take all the help we can get. If Dad stops by here first, tell him we already went over to the house."

"Will do," Meghan replied, as she headed to the kitchen.

With impeccable timing, Todd pulled onto the property just as Aiden was parking his pickup. The small crew immediately unloaded the tools from the back of Aiden's truck and got to work. It didn't take Bailey and Emma long to figure out what they could do that would help the most. They held the siding boards in place while the guys nailed them up. Before long everyone had gotten into a good flow and the siding went up quickly. Once the lower boards had been installed on the back wall, Aiden and Matt rolled the scaffolding into place so they could continue working their way up the wall with the siding. Todd remained on the ground, handing the pieces of siding up to Aiden and Matt who were working from the scaffolding.

"Hey," Emma called from the ground, "can I climb up and work on the scaffolding too? I feel kind of useless down here."

Matt looked at Aiden, then both men looked down at Todd.

"What do you think, Dad?" Aiden asked.

Todd looked over at Emma, who wore a hopeful smile on her face. "I don't see why not," he said. "She's wearing a hard hat and a smile. Both admirable qualities for a construction worker."

Emma pumped her fist in the air and yelled, "Yes!" Then she

wasted no time climbing up the side of the scaffolding to join Matt and Aiden.

Aiden chuckled and said, "It's probably safer with two people working up here, rather than three. Matt, why don't you and Emma work up here while Dad hands siding up to you? Bailey and I can start the lower boards on the next wall."

"Sounds like a good plan to me," Matt replied as he smiled at Emma.

Todd stayed busy handing siding to everyone, but he wasn't too busy to notice how well the young couples worked together. The girls had caught on quickly and seemed to truly enjoy helping out. Neither of them was afraid of hard work, and they both willingly helped wherever they could. By the time the sun began to set, quickly making it too dark to work, a fair part of the back of the house now had siding installed.

Matt and Emma climbed down from the scaffolding while Aiden and Bailey gathered tools and loaded them back into Aiden's truck. Todd walked over to the group of tired workers while they stood back and marveled at all they had accomplished in a few short hours.

"You four sure work well together," Todd said, nodding his head toward the house. "That's quite a night's work. Why don't you call it a night?"

Emma stood next to her sister and said, "Look at that, Bales. Can you believe we learned how to install siding tonight? And it was a lot of fun!"

"I know," Bailey said in agreement. "Can't you just hear Mom now? You did *what*?"

The girls laughed as they started walking back across the property.

"We'll see you guys tomorrow," Bailey called back to Aiden and Matt. "It's time for a shower, then I plan to fall into bed. I'm a pastor. I'm not used to all this manual labor."

Todd laughed as he walked to his truck. "I'll be sure to tell Travis that!"

Bailey just laughed and kept walking.

* * *

After the young adults called it quits for the night, Todd still wasn't quite ready to head home, so he went next door and joined Travis and Meghan on the back deck. They were enjoying the beautiful weather with a cold glass of iced tea. Todd poured himself a glass of tea, grabbed a chocolate chip cookie from the plate, and pulled up a chair.

"You guys should have seen those kids tonight," Todd said. "You never would have guessed those girls had never done that kind of work before. They caught on real quick. Those four work well together – they make a great team."

"I think it's wonderful the girls show such an interest in what the boys are doing," Meghan added. "That's important to the guys."

Travis looked out across the backyard with a smile on his face. "I get the feeling there's a lot more than friendship developing between them. I know Matt and Emma have been hitting the batting cages before work occasionally. And Aiden stops by the church nearly every day to take Bailey out for lunch. She told me sometimes they just go to the park and eat a lunch that Aiden packed for them."

"I wonder if Aiden and Bailey were more than friends in the Army," Todd said to no one in particular.

Travis looked over at Todd and replied, "I asked him about that when Bailey was here for the interview. He said they were good friends and went to lunch occasionally, but he wasn't sure that was really considered dating."

Meghan said, "I'm not sure they ever admitted it to each other, or to themselves, but I get the feeling they were attracted to each other even back then. I think running into each other after two years may have given them a little push."

"Well, sis," Todd said to Meghan, "I, for one, would be happy as a clam if both those young ladies joined our family."

Meghan nodded her head in agreement. "I agree, Todd. I think we all would."

* * *

When the weekend rolled around, there was once again a small but growing crew hard at work on the house. Todd and Travis were nearly always working with Aiden and Matt, along with a few volunteers from the construction company. Occasionally, some of the teenagers from the youth center would stop by to lend a hand as well. It was no longer unusual to find Bailey and Emma working right alongside the others to complete the house.

The most welcome surprise of all, at least in Matt's eyes, was his dad. John had not had an easy time of it during his rehab and recovery. Added to that was the fact he had been out of the workforce for several years because of his addictions. Seeing the change in him after the house fire amazed nearly everyone. But Matt was the one most surprised by the transformation. He had all but given up hope of ever having a positive relationship with his father. Yet here they were, working alongside each other almost every day. John had become an eager student and was quickly becoming a valuable part of the construction team.

Matt walked up behind his dad, who was setting up some sawhorses on the front side of the house.

Putting his hand on his dad's back to get his attention, Matt asked, "Hey, Dad, do you want to continue helping with the siding and trim today? Or would you rather help build the front deck and porch?"

John looked up at his son with pride in his eyes. "You're going to build the deck today?"

"Well," Matt replied, "some of us are going to get started on the front part so it's easier to get in and out of the house. We'll finish the wrap-around and the back deck in a few days."

"I'd sure like to help out on the deck and see how that's done," John replied hopefully. "If it's okay with you and Aiden."

"Sure," Matt said with a smile. "We can use another good set of hands."

"If I haven't said so recently, son," John began, "thanks again for not giving up on me. I really like doing this construction stuff. It gives a person a sense of accomplishment when you can see the progress."

"I agree," Matt said with a nod. "That's one of the things I like about it too. You've been a big help, Dad. Once you put your mind to it, you have been learning new things quickly. Well, I'm going to go round up the guys who will be working on the deck. I'll be right back, then we can get started."

Work continued on the house throughout the day, with a tremendous amount of progress being made. Since most of the siding had already been installed earlier, it didn't take long to wrap that up and finish the outside trim. While Matt, his dad, and a couple guys from the construction company worked on the front deck, Aiden took some others inside to begin putting up drywall. Travis and Todd had completed most of the electrical work earlier in the week, and the inspector had signed off on that part of the project.

Mike Slater had made it his personal mission to keep the workers fed. Whenever a crew was putting in a full day at the construction site, he made a point to stop by at lunchtime with pizza and cold drinks. This day was no different. Right on schedule, Mike came by to deliver food and drinks for lunch. JC and Amy stopped by as well to marvel at the progress on what would become their home. Although they didn't stay long during lunch, JC had promised he and Amy would stop back by at the end of the day. With Amy in the third trimester of her pregnancy, she tired easily.

By the time Aiden and Matt convinced their hard-working volunteers to call it quits for the day, everyone was exhausted. The crew had gathered at the front of the house to discuss their progress. Other than painting the siding, and building the rest of the deck, the outside of the house was pretty much complete. Focus was now turning to the interior, where drywall installation was well underway. Todd had taken charge of coordinating inspections with the city so construction wouldn't be held up.

As Aiden and Matt were discussing a basic schedule for the next few days, JC's Jeep pulled onto the property. JC walked around to the passenger side and helped Amy out of the vehicle. He then reached into the back and brought out a box before they walked up to the tired workers.

JC sat the open box on the tailgate of one of the pickups and said, "Amy made a big batch of cupcakes for everyone. Help yourselves."

Everyone gathered around to grab a cupcake.

"Thanks, sis," Matt said. "This is great!"

"It's not much," Amy replied. "Just a little something to show how much we appreciate everything you all are doing. Especially knowing a lot of you are volunteering in your free time when you could be doing something a lot more fun."

"I don't know, Amy," Emma replied, "Bailey and I are having a blast helping out on the house."

"And it gets us outside," Bailey added. "With our jobs being primarily indoors, it's nice to be outside working and getting some fresh air."

"Well," Aiden added with a laugh, "I'm not sure how fresh the air is on a construction site, but the scenery is certainly a lot better these days."

"I have to agree with you, Aiden," Matt said with a smile as he reached over and wiped some dirt off Emma's cheek. "The scenery is much better."

Chapter Ten

Life had gotten so busy for everyone that they had to constantly remind each other to slow down and take a break occasionally. Matt was very driven to get the house finished before Amy had her baby, even though Todd continually reminded him that it wouldn't be the end of the world if that didn't happen. Somehow, to get the boys to slow down a bit so they didn't burn themselves out, Travis and Meghan had convinced everyone to take a break to go to a mid-week baseball game.

Seated in the stands along the third-base line, Travis and his family took up a large section of the bleachers. Travis and Meghan were joined by not only JC and Amy, but also Kaci, Jason, and the twins, who had insisted on inviting Mr. Mike to the game as well. Todd and his wife Nicole sat behind the twins, who always managed to grab the spot on either side of Mike. Aiden and Bailey sat beside Matt and Emma at the end of the row. With hotdogs and drinks in hand, everyone settled in to watch the Hope Angels play their league rivals, the Rainier Bears.

Toward the end of the game, the Hope fans were cheering loudly after their team executed a difficult double play that prevented the Bears from pulling ahead on the scoreboard. Matt reached over and gave Aaron a high five.

"That was an awesome play, wasn't it, Aaron?" Matt asked.

"It sure was!" Aaron agreed.

Mike turned to Sophie and asked, "Are you and Aaron playing Little League again this year, Sophie?"

"Yeah, it's so much fun!" Sophie replied enthusiastically.

"What position do you play, Sophie?" Mike asked.

"I play center field on our team," Sophie said proudly.

"What about you, Aaron?" Mike asked.

Aaron beamed as he looked over at Matt. "I'm the shortstop, just like Uncle Matt. I'm going to be as good as he was in high school."

"Is that right?" Mike asked. "You're going to have to work hard then because Matt was a pretty good shortstop."

"I know," Aaron said seriously. "I've been practicing with Dad, and with Uncle Matt when he has time."

Matt reached over and patted Aaron on the shoulder. "He works hard, Mike. I think someday he'll be a great shortstop. And Sophie does a fantastic job in center field. There's not much that gets past her."

"Well," Mike said with a knowing smile, "there's no doubt baseball is in their blood."

About that time, the Hope batter hit a long ball over the right-field fence, scoring the two runners on base. By the end of the game, the Angels finished on top, beating the Bears by three runs, much to the delight of the hometown fans.

The mid-week break was just what everyone needed to have a chance to regroup. After the game, they all gathered at the ice cream parlor, where Mike insisted on treating them to ice cream.

Sophie thanked Mike for the ice cream and said, "Baseball is hard work!"

Everyone laughed and Emma patted Sophie on the shoulder and said, "But you weren't playing, Sophie."

"I know," replied the little girl dramatically. "But even watching baseball is hard work!" Then, pointing to Mike enjoying an ice cream sundae, Sophie added, "See, even Mr. Mike needed ice cream!"

"You might just have a point there, Sophie," Emma said nodding. "It's a good thing Mr. Mike invited us along for ice cream then."

"I know," Sophie nodded seriously. "Without ice cream, we wouldn't have the strength to get home!"

* * *

When Emma heard JC and Amy talking about an upcoming concert in the park, she knew she didn't want to miss it. The sisters had fallen in love with that community park the first time they saw it, and she knew Bailey would want to go.

Later that afternoon, Emma went looking for JC. She heard beautiful sounds coming from the music room down the hall at the youth center, so she was sure that was where she would find him. She opened the door quietly and stood just inside the room listening to the music. When JC stopped at the end of the song, Emma walked up to him at the piano and put her hand on his shoulder.

"Another one of your compositions, JC?" she asked him as he smiled.

"Yeah," he replied. "I actually just finished this one a few days ago. Did you like it?"

"JC, I love all your original compositions," Emma replied sincerely. "You are very gifted."

"Whatever gift I have comes from God," JC replied humbly.

"I didn't want to interrupt you, but I had a question," Emma said.

"Sure," JC replied. "What's up?"

"I overheard you and Amy talking about a concert in the park coming up soon," Emma said. "Can you tell me a little about it? I know Bailey and I would love to go."

"It's a lot of fun," JC replied with a smile. "We usually have three or four concerts in the park every year. Most of the time they're just local groups from around the area. They play all kinds of music. Folk is really popular, as well as country and some rock music. And they have food booths scattered throughout the park as well. All the concerts are free to the public, too."

"That's great!" Emma said enthusiastically. "I'll be sure to tell Bailey so we can go. I assume you and Amy are going?"

"Oh, we never miss them," JC said. "The concerts in the park have a lot of wonderful memories for me and Amy. We had our first dance under one of the big oak trees in that park."

"That is so cool!" Emma said. "Do you happen to know if Matt ever goes to those concerts?"

JC smiled as he replied, "Matt usually doesn't miss them. And I'm quite sure he doesn't plan to miss this one."

"Really?" Emma asked hopefully.

"Really," JC replied. In the short time Emma had been working at JC's Hope, JC had come to view her as a sister, and her happiness was important to him.

"Can I ask you something as a friend, Emma?" JC began.

"Sure," she replied.

"You and Bailey have been helping Aiden and Matt over at the house quite a bit. And I know you and Matt have been hitting the batting cages before work occasionally. You like Matt, don't you?"

Emma blushed slightly before replying. "Yeah, I really do. He's so nice, and he's easy to talk to. We have a lot in common too." Emma chuckled softly before adding, "And he's cute."

JC laughed and said, "If I had a nickel for every girl who said that when he was in high school and used to hang out here, I'd be a rich man!

"You know, Emma," JC continued, "Matt really likes you too. And I have it on very good authority that he plans to ask you to go to the concert with him."

"He does?" Emma asked with excitement. "How do you know?"

"You remember I'm married to his sister, right?" JC chuckled.

Emma laughed as she slapped her forehead. "Oh, right! I'm still new enough here that I sometimes forget how everyone's related. You're Aiden's cousin, right?"

"Yep," JC confirmed.

Emma stalled for a moment before plunging in with her next question. "And you and Aiden are pretty close, right?"

"You could say that," JC answered. "We grew up being best friends and cousins, and we're nearly the same age."

"So, do you happen to know if he likes Bailey?" Emma asked with a smile.

"Emma," JC replied with a nod, "I know for a fact Aiden is crazy about your sister. But you did *not* hear that from me!"

"Hear what?" Emma asked innocently as they both laughed. "And you definitely did *not* hear me say that Bailey is just as crazy about Aiden!"

* * *

The sounds of music from several bands floated through town and mingled with the smell of fair food as the concert in the park was in full swing. Picnic tables were scattered throughout the park, and people brought their own blankets and lawn chairs so they could sit wherever they wanted. Travis and his family had set up camp under one of the large oak trees near the center of the park. That served as their base camp as family and friends meandered through the park to listen to the different bands and sample food from various booths.

Travis, Meghan, Todd, and Nicole were sitting in lawn chairs enjoying the shade of the large tree. Kaci and Jason kept an eye on the twins from their blanket on the ground. Although, in reality, Aaron and Sophie spent most of their time entertaining Mr. Mike and leading him on a journey to investigate all the food booths.

"There they are," Meghan said, waving toward the parking lot.

Jason jumped up and said, "I'll go see if they need help carrying anything."

Within minutes, the small entourage had gathered lawn chairs and blankets, along with a small cooler, from their vehicles and were headed toward the rest of the family. Aiden and Matt spread a couple of blankets on the ground, then set up two lawn chairs. Jason set up a chair for Amy, and JC immediately helped his very pregnant wife into the chair.

"How are you doing, Amy?" Meghan asked with concern.

"Oh, I'm doing fine, Meghan," Amy replied with a smile, as she patted her belly. "I just get tired easily. This little munchkin appears to be a night owl and keeps me up half the night."

Travis chuckled as he said, "I seem to remember Josh kept his mom up most of the night too."

"Oh, great!" Amy replied with a laugh. "At least I have someone to blame!"

Matt walked into the middle of the group, with his hands tucked into the front pockets of his Levis, and casually asked, "So, when are we checking out the food?"

Todd laughed and said, "Sorry, buddy, you're too late. Aaron and Sophie captured Mike earlier and took him on a tour. I'm sure by now they've cleaned out all the food!"

"Not on my watch, they don't!" Matt said as he reached for Emma's hand. "Come on, Emma, let's see if we can get ahead of those kids.

"Aiden," Matt continued, "are you and Bailey coming?"

"Right behind you, buddy!" Aiden replied as he helped Bailey up from the blanket.

Everyone laughed as the four took off running toward the food booths.

"I'm glad those two boys are taking a little time away from the house project to have fun," Meghan said.

"Matt is so concerned about having the house finished before the baby arrives," Todd said. "I keep reminding him that it'll be fine."

JC laughed and said, "Amy and I keep telling him the same thing. We don't want them working themselves into the ground to meet a self-imposed deadline."

Travis looked over at JC and Amy and asked with a laugh, "So, do you two have any inside information on those four? They've sure been spending a lot of time together."

"I know Matt really likes Emma," JC said. "And she told me the other day that she likes him. I think they're good for each other."

"I agree," Amy added with a smile. "Emma is always asking me things about Matt, like she wants to know everything about him and what makes him tick."

"Aiden holds his cards pretty close to his chest where Bailey is concerned," Todd said. "But all you have to do is watch him when they're together and there's no doubt he cares for her. A lot."

JC chuckled before saying, "Okay, you did *not* hear this from me. But Emma also told me the other day that Bailey is crazy about Aiden. And I happen to know he feels the same way about her."

"Boy, you're just a wealth of information, son," Travis said with a laugh.

Kaci laughed as she looked around the circle at her family. "You guys sound like a bunch of gossiping old hens! Let them find their own way, and we'll all just meet up at the wedding!"

With that, they all laughed and settled back to enjoy the music.

Chapter Eleven

Business had been hectic and steady at Byers Construction all morning. Aiden, Matt, and some of the other employees had been coming in early all week in an effort to stay on top of things. Matt had just finished loading another truck with lumber, the fourth one this morning, then parked the forklift alongside the building. Aiden finished taking another order from a contractor just as Todd and Matt walked in the back door shortly before noon.

Todd walked up and put his arm around Aiden's shoulder.

"Did you get Jake taken care of, son?" Todd asked.

"Yeah," Aiden replied. "We got his urgent order placed, but he said he would be back tomorrow with a larger order."

"Does it look like we have everything he needs for the urgent order?" Todd asked.

"Yeah," Aiden replied. "Not a problem."

"You boys have been here for several hours already this morning," Todd said, looking at Aiden and Matt. "Why don't you take a little longer lunch break today to catch your breath."

"You don't have to tell me twice!" Matt said with a laugh. "I'm going to swing by the center. Emma was hoping I could spot her on the rock-climbing wall during lunch."

Todd chuckled. "Don't forget to eat some lunch while you're

out, or you're going to be mighty hungry by the end of the day."

"You know me, Todd," Matt said with a grin, "how often do I forget to eat? I'll probably stop and pick up something from the deli on my way over to the center."

Aiden looked at Matt and smiled. "It looks like I'll follow you to the deli then. I was planning to stop there to grab something for lunch in the park with Bailey."

Todd watched the young men walk out to their trucks and silently thanked God for bringing Bailey and Emma into their lives.

* * *

Matt picked up lunch at the deli, then rushed over to JC's Hope to meet up with Emma. Pulling into the parking lot, he noticed JC's Jeep and hoped he would have a chance to say hi to him. He hurried into the center, which opened into the spacious gym, and spotted Emma near the rock wall, talking to a teenage girl.

Matt walked up to the girls and smiled at Emma. "Hi, Emma," he said.

"Hi, Matt," Emma replied. Then turning to the teenager, she said, "Kristen, this is Matt."

Matt reached out to shake the girl's hand and said, "Hi, Kristen. It's nice to meet you."

"Hi, Matt," Kristen said with a smile. "Well, I'd better get going. Nice to meet you, Matt. I'll talk to you later, Emma."

Matt held up a small cooler and said, "I brought lunch from the deli. Do you want to eat first, or climb first?"

"As long as the lunch is good in the cooler," Emma replied, "why don't we do the climbing first? Thanks for coming by to spot me. I can't wait to see how high I can get on the wall."

Matt sat the cooler off to the side and assisted Emma in

getting into the rock-climbing harness. After making sure everything was fastened securely, he smiled and asked, "Are you ready to go?"

"Let's do this!" Emma replied enthusiastically.

Matt grabbed hold of the rope as Emma began climbing. She quickly climbed the first few feet, then was more cautious as she began to get higher on the wall. With slow, steady climbing, it wasn't long before she was nearing the top of the fifteen-foot wall. She started to look down and wavered a bit.

"Don't look down, Emma," Matt cautioned. "Just keep looking ahead at your hand and foot holds. You're only a couple feet from the top of the wall. You can do it, Emma. Slow and steady."

A few more moves and Emma reached the top of the wall. "Down," she called to Matt on the ground.

Matt guided the rope as Emma began rappelling down the wall. Once she touched the ground, wearing a huge smile, she wrapped Matt in a victory hug.

"I did it!" she said happily. "I made it all the way to the top! Coming down the wall was so much fun!"

Matt couldn't help but get wrapped up in her excitement. "You were great, Emma! Was that the first time you've climbed to the top of the wall?"

"Yep!" she replied, as she reached over and gave Matt a quick kiss on the cheek.

"Let's get you out of the harness," Matt said, "then we can sit down and eat. I think you may have earned your lunch."

"You bet I did!" Emma said, still smiling. "I'm starved!"

"Now you sound like me," Matt said with a laugh. He picked up the cooler, took Emma by the hand, and walked over to a table along the wall. "I hope you like turkey sandwiches. I brought us each a sandwich and some potato salad. I'll go grab a couple bottles of water from the kitchen."

While eating their lunch, Matt noticed Mike Slater walk in and go straight to the baseball arcade game. He yelled over to Mike, "Hey, Mike! Save a game for me!"

Mike waved in Matt's direction and replied, "Finish your lunch, son, then I'll challenge you to a game."

Emma and Matt ate in silence for a few moments. She looked across the table at Matt and said, "You're pretty close with a lot of the people from the center, aren't you, Matt?"

Matt looked around the room and said quietly, "This place saved me, Emma. I don't know where I would have ended up without JC's Hope and the people here. JC and Mike took me in and made me feel like family right from the beginning. And Mike has contributed so much to the center. He's the one who supplied all those arcade games and the laptops down in the classrooms. He also supplied the piano and keyboard in the music room. He's amazing."

"I knew he gifted the building and property to JC for the center," Emma said. "And he's still dropping by all the time to see if we need anything. I didn't realize he donated the games and laptops too. And even instruments, wow. But it shouldn't surprise me. He's incredible."

"When JC and Todd started the apprenticeship program at the high school," Matt continued, "Todd took me under his wing and taught me everything I know about construction. Which, compared to him and his family, is almost nothing. But it's a lot more than I knew before. Todd is like a dad to me. I have so much respect for him. He was there for me when I really needed someone. I can never repay him for that."

Emma reached over and put her hand on Matt's forearm. "You're repaying him every day, Matt. When he looks at you and sees the man you've turned into, that's the only thanks he'll ever need. Todd, Travis, Meghan, and their entire family are amazing people. We're both so lucky to have them in our lives."

"That's a fact," Matt agreed. "Like Travis always likes to say, 'God is good. All the time.' And he's certainly right about that."

Matt stood and gathered their trash, then took Emma by the hand. "Let's go see if I can beat Mike at that baseball game. Eventually, someone has to beat that man!"

Walking up behind Mike, Matt put his hand on his back and said, "Okay, Mike, let's do this. Do you want to go first, or do you want me to?"

Mike laughed and asked, "Do you feel lucky today, Matt?"

"Yep," Matt laughed. "It's my day. You're going down, Mike. Why don't you go first so I know what score I have to beat."

Mike played his round of the game and finished with an incredibly high score. He turned to Matt with a smile and said, "So, are you still feeling lucky?"

Matt moved up to the arcade game with a determined look on his face and said with more confidence than he felt, "Piece of cake. I've got this."

At the end of Matt's game, they both looked at his total score. Although a great game, it was several thousand points below Mike's score.

Matt stepped away from the machine shaking his head. He took a theatrical bow and said, "I bow to the master. You're amazing, Mike."

Mike just laughed and said, "I may be nearly seventy, but I've still got some good moves. Keep practicing, Matt, and we'll have a rematch one of these days."

With that and a chuckle, Mike patted Matt on the back and headed out the door, leaving the young man shaking his head once again.

Matt reached for Emma's hand and said, "I've got to get back to work. Maybe I'll see you later?"

"Yeah, me too," Emma said. "I'll give you a call when I get off work."

Matt pulled her into a hug, and they shared a quick kiss before they went their separate ways.

JC was just coming down the hallway from his office and he smiled at Emma as she passed him. He walked up to Matt and patted him on the back.

"I was hoping I would get a chance to at least say hi to you today," JC said. "I'm glad you were able to stop by. Emma's been talking about that wall all morning. How did it go?"

"She made it to the top of the wall," Matt said with a smile. "She was so excited!"

"Good for her!" JC replied. "It was good seeing you, Matt, but I'll let you go. I know you need to get back to work."

"Take it easy, JC," Matt said, as he headed toward the door.

* * *

Travis happened to be in the foyer of the church when Aiden stopped by.

"Hi, Aiden," Travis said in greeting. "I was wondering if you'd be coming by today."

"Hi, Uncle Travis," Aiden replied with a smile. "Is Bailey around? I told her I'd take her to the park for lunch today."

"She's back in the office," Travis said, nodding. "I'm sure she's probably expecting you. I'm headed out for a meeting. You kids enjoy your lunch. It's a beautiful day for a picnic at the park."

Just as Aiden was walking through the sanctuary toward the pastor's office, he noticed that Bailey had already left the office and was walking toward him.

"Hi, Aiden," she greeted with a smile. "I'm ready to head to the park if you are. I've been inside, looking out the window daydreaming all morning. I'm ready for some of that fresh air."

"Then let's not waste any time," Aiden replied as he took her by the hand. "I stopped at the deli and picked up some lunch, so we can just relax and enjoy the nice weather."

As soon as Aiden pulled into a parking space at the park, he hurried around and opened the passenger door of his pickup and helped Bailey out. Grabbing the bag with their lunch, he started to reach behind the passenger seat.

"Do you want to sit at a picnic table, or on a blanket on the ground?" he asked. "I'm fine either way."

She took the bag of food from him and replied, "Let's sit on the ground with a blanket. That feels more like a picnic."

Aiden grabbed the blanket from behind the seat, closed the door, and took Bailey's free hand. After walking toward the center of the park, Aiden spread the blanket on the ground in the shade of one of the large oak trees and they both got comfortable.

Bailey reached for the lunch sack and peered inside. "So, what did you bring us for lunch?"

"I got you a turkey, bacon, and Swiss sandwich on sourdough bread and a side of potato salad," Aiden replied with a smile.

Bailey looked across the blanket at him and asked, "How did you know that was my favorite sandwich?"

"Whenever we happened to have lunch together on the base, that's what you ordered," Aiden replied, smiling.

"And you remembered that from over two years ago? I'm impressed."

Aiden simply smiled and dug into the bag for his tuna sandwich. The two ate in relative silence, enjoying the weather and the opportunity to relax. After finishing his sandwich and potato salad, Aiden stretched out on the blanket, put his arms behind his neck, and stared up at the clouds.

"Do you ever just stare at the clouds, Bailey?" he asked, looking over at her.

"Are you kidding me?" Bailey asked incredulously. "I've done that my entire life. I used to lay in the grass in the park back home and just stare up at the sky for what seemed like hours. It's so peaceful and relaxing."

Moving over beside Aiden, she continued, "You know, I've come here to the park by myself a few times. Just to lay in the grass, stare at the clouds, and unwind."

"You have?" Aiden asked as he looked at her.

"Sure," she replied, stretching out beside him. "I love this park. It reminds me of all the good memories from my childhood before we moved to the city."

Aiden rolled onto his side so he could look at Bailey and propped his head on his hand. "Life has been so crazy busy the past few months. Have I told you how glad I am that God brought you to Hope?"

Bailey smiled before answering. "Not in so many words. But I could tell. I'm glad too."

Aiden sat upright on the blanket and crossed his legs, looking at Bailey. She sat up as well and crossed her legs, so they were facing each other.

Aiden reached over and took both her hands in his. "You have no idea how surprised I was to see you at the church that day. You could have knocked me over with a feather."

"Me too," Bailey said quietly. "I could barely talk. To see you again after two years…" she trailed off. "I never thought I would see you again." Her eyes began to mist over.

"Can I ask you something, Bailey?" Aiden said.

She just nodded.

"When we were in the Army together," Aiden began, "and you were counseling my buddy Drake, so we ran into each other frequently, were you interested in me at all? I mean, I know we became friends and went to lunch together occasionally. But did you look at me as another soldier who just happened to be a friend?"

"No," Bailey responded softly, squeezing his hand. "I don't know how to explain it really. But the first time we met I knew you were someone special. I was instantly attracted to you and wasn't sure how to deal with that. I've never had that happen before."

Aiden smiled and squeezed both her hands. "You have no idea how happy that makes me. I felt the same way and wasn't sure what to do about it. In the Army, you never knew when you may be transferred, so I didn't want to take a chance of getting too close and then having one of us transferred out. It was easier to keep a distance."

"I know," Bailey agreed.

"We're not in the Army anymore," Aiden said quietly.

"No, we aren't," Bailey replied.

"I'm not going to be transferred out of Hope," he continued.

"I don't think I am either," Bailey said, never breaking eye contact. "I think God has stationed me here permanently."

Aiden started to stand and reached to help Bailey up as well. "God knows what He's doing. I'm not going to argue with Him."

"Me neither," Bailey whispered, as Aiden pulled her close into his arms.

"God is good," Aiden said softly, tipping his head down and looking into her eyes.

"All the time," Bailey replied quietly.

Then their lips met in a tender kiss as they marveled over God's infinite wisdom.

Chapter Twelve

Over the next several weeks, tremendous progress was made on the interior of the house. All the drywall had been installed, taping and texturing were finished, plumbing and electrical were complete, and some of the cabinets had been installed. The only major tasks remaining were the painting and flooring. Throughout the entire construction, Matt's dad had been on site working alongside the others nearly every time someone was at the house. He had proven to be a hard worker and a quick learner, and he seemed to genuinely enjoy the work.

Aiden, Todd, and John were waiting at the house for Matt to arrive with the interior paint. JC and Amy had picked up paint samples a few days ago and were finally able to settle on the interior colors. The exterior of the house was a different story. JC seemed to have no preference for the color of the house, and Amy was struggling with indecision. She told Josh it was "pregnancy brain" and not her fault. So, the exterior of the house was prepped and ready to paint, awaiting the final color decision. In the meantime, the interior painting would start as soon as Matt arrived.

John walked over to Aiden and Todd and asked, "Do you know which room we're going to start painting first? I can spread out tarps and get things set up if you want me to."

Todd put his hand on John's shoulder and replied, "That would be great, John. I can help you. I think we'll probably start in the living room." Turning to Aiden, he asked, "What do you think, son?"

"Yeah," Aiden said, "that's what Matt and I decided last night. Let's go ahead and get things set up. Matt should be here in a few minutes."

A short time later, Matt pulled onto the lot in his pickup, followed by JC and Amy in their Jeep. Matt unloaded a small hand truck from the back of the pickup and began unloading five-gallon buckets of paint. The others came out of the house as soon as they heard Matt's truck, so it didn't take long to unload everything.

JC helped Amy out of the Jeep, and they started walking toward the house. "Amy wanted to see the inside of the house again before we started the painting," JC said as they walked inside. "She thought it would be nice to have some more before and after pictures."

John walked up to his daughter, put his hand on her arm, and asked, "How are you feeling, Amy? Are you doing okay?"

"I'm fine, Dad," she replied with a smile. "This last month certainly lives up to everyone's warnings. I'm ready for this pregnancy to be over."

"You only have a few more weeks, right?" John asked.

"The doctor said probably about three weeks," Amy answered.

Matt had been standing next to Todd a few feet away. "So, we need to hurry and get this house finished," he said.

Todd patted Matt on the back and said, "It will get finished when it gets finished, Matt. Don't keep worrying about it."

JC looked at Matt and added, "Uncle Todd is right, Matt. It's not a big deal if the house is finished before the baby arrives. We've already talked to Mike, and Bailey and Emma plan to take over the lease on our apartment. So, everyone is very flexible. We'll move when the house is finished. By the way, you guys, the house looks great! You've done a fantastic job on it, especially since you've been building it in your spare time. Amy and I can't begin to thank you. You guys are unbelievable."

Matt walked over and shook JC's hand. "It has been an honor to build our first house for you and Amy. That's what family does." Then he winked at his sister and added, "Besides, if it falls apart you can always tell people, 'Well, what can you expect from a free house?'"

Amy reached over and smacked her brother on the arm and said, "Don't give up your day job, Matt. I don't think you'd make it as a comedian."

Everyone laughed as JC and Amy started walking through the house, and the others began opening paint buckets.

As the painting was set to begin, Todd walked up to JC and Amy to catch them before they left. "Have you two settled on colors for the exterior of the house yet?" Todd asked.

JC looked at his wife and smiled. "Not yet. Amy's having a tough time deciding."

Amy nudged JC's shoulder and replied with a chuckle, "Well, you certainly haven't been any help."

"I told you I would be happy with whatever colors you choose," JC replied with a smile. "It honestly doesn't matter to me."

"That still doesn't help, honey," Amy said with a smile.

Todd chuckled at the exchange, then said, "I have an idea that might help, Amy. Why don't you have Meghan help you choose? She has a good eye for design and colors. You could ask her to go to the paint store with you to look at samples. I'm sure with her help you won't have any trouble deciding on something you'll all like."

"That's a great idea, Todd!" Amy said happily. "I don't know why I didn't think of that."

"Must be that pregnancy brain again," JC said chuckling.

Amy slapped JC on the arm and said, "Watch it, buster, or I'll have them paint the house hot pink and royal purple!"

"No, please don't!" JC laughed. "I surrender! No more comments about pregnancy brain, I promise."

"That's more like it," Amy said with satisfaction. "Now, Mr. Harmon, why don't you take me home so I can get off my feet for a while."

"Yes, ma'am!" JC replied quickly.

"Todd," Amy began, "I'll talk to Meghan and get paint chips to either you or Matt very soon."

"Sounds good, Amy," Todd said. "I'll let Matt know."

Then, turning to JC with a smile, he said, "JC, take your wife home and let her rest. We have work to do! It might not hurt to stop at the florist and pick up some flowers for her too. You really dug yourself into a hole there, buddy."

JC laughed as he helped his wife to the Jeep, and Todd chuckled as he walked toward the living room to help with the painting.

With Todd and Aiden doing the cut-in for painting the walls, and Matt and John using rollers to paint the bulk of the walls, the job was going fairly quickly. They were nearly finished with the living room when Travis showed up. Having an extra set of experienced hands made things go even quicker. Before long they had crews painting in two different rooms. By the time they quit for the day, more than half the interior of the house had been painted. Another good day and the interior painting would be finished.

The men all gathered in the living room area and sat down in some folding chairs to discuss their game plan for the rest of the work.

"Wow," Aiden said, looking around the room with satisfaction, "we got a lot done today. It won't take long to finish the interior painting. Should we go ahead and schedule the installation for the rest of the cabinets? I think we could get the guys here tomorrow or the next day."

Matt looked to Todd and Travis for direction. "What do you think?"

"I think that's certainly reasonable," Todd replied. "Even if they were able to do it tomorrow, all the painting is finished in the rooms that still need cabinets installed, so that won't be a problem. The sooner, the better."

"I agree," said Matt. "Then that just leaves the flooring, right? Or am I missing something?"

"No, you're right," Aiden replied. "We just need to install flooring and do any final touch-ups, and the interior will be finished."

"Does anyone know what they've decided to do for flooring?" Travis asked.

"Aiden and I talked to Amy a couple nights ago," Matt said. "Even though they both like the looks of the hardwood laminate flooring, they think it would be best to carpet most of the house. They thought that would cut down on falls when the baby starts learning to walk since hardwood flooring can get slippery."

"That's smart thinking," Travis agreed. "Have they picked out carpeting yet, or flooring for the kitchen, bathrooms, and laundry room?"

"Yeah," Aiden answered. "JC gave me their samples last night, so we got the flooring ordered this morning. Everything is in stock, so we won't have to wait on anything."

"Impressive," Todd said, nodding his head. "You two have done a great job coordinating things and making it all come together."

"Now if we could only get my sister to decide what color she wants the outside of her house painted," Matt said with mock annoyance, "that would certainly help."

"The house will be finished before you know it," Travis said. "Which brings up another point. I keep forgetting to ask Josh how they're doing with packing to be ready for the move. I know Amy shouldn't be doing much packing. Have any of you guys talked to them about that?"

"Actually," John began, "I've been stopping by their apartment nearly every day to pack things up for them."

Everyone looked at him in amazement.

"Really, Dad?" Matt asked. "Amy never mentioned that."

John looked at the floor before replying. "I asked her not to. I figured it was the least I could do. You guys have all been working on the house in what you call your free time, after working at your full-time jobs. That applies to Todd and Travis too. I don't have a full-time job during the day, so it's not like I'm doing much unless you guys are over here working on the house. Besides, I felt like I owed it to her. Let's face it, I was never a great dad to you kids. Heck, I wasn't even a mediocre dad. So, I have a lot to make up for. The least I can do is get those kids packed up so they're ready to move when the house is finished."

Matt stood and walked over to his dad and pulled him into a hug. By the time the hug was released, both men had tears in their eyes.

"I'm proud of you, Dad," Matt said sincerely. "You've been making a lot of positive changes and trying to make up for past mistakes. That's not easy, but you're doing it. The future will be great for you. It's never too late to make changes."

"Thanks, son," John replied. "That means a lot coming from you."

"So, how much of their stuff is packed up?" Matt asked. "Do you need some help?"

John chuckled and said, "The only things I haven't packed are what they use every day. Amy kept laughing and telling me to make sure I left clothes unpacked so they had something to wear."

Everyone laughed and shook their heads at the surprising development.

"Well," Todd said with a chuckle, "I guess we can stop worrying about getting them ready to move. Sounds like John is already in charge of that. Once the house is finished, it sounds like they'll be able to move in with very little effort."

"Why don't we call it a day," Aiden suggested. "The finish line is in sight."

"As long as there are chocolate chip cookies at that finish line," Matt laughed, "I'll be able to keep my eyes on the prize!"

Todd slapped Matt playfully on the back and said, "Don't ever change, Matt. Don't ever change."

* * *

The next two weeks were insanely busy as the final work on the house continued. The interior was completely painted, and the cabinetry had been installed. Todd and Travis installed tile flooring in the kitchen, laundry room, and both bathrooms. They left the carpet installation to the professionals. Even though both men were competent when it came to installing carpet, they admitted the experts would be able to finish the job faster. With the occasional help of Bailey and Emma, Matt and Aiden had gone through the entire house to do whatever small touch-ups needed to be done. John was a huge help in keeping the areas tidy and gathering tools. All in all, the makeshift crew worked very well together and had gotten into a pattern that seemed to work for them.

Standing in the living room, looking around the finished house with satisfaction, the men were all smiles. Suddenly they heard a car door slam out front and footsteps hurrying up the porch. The front door opened with a flourish and Meghan stood there with a huge smile on her face, holding paint chips in her hand.

"We did it!" she exclaimed excitedly. "We finished the final piece of the puzzle! The exterior colors have been chosen!"

Cheers erupted in the room. You would have thought someone just won the lottery.

"So, sis," Todd said, "don't keep us in suspense. What colors did you two ladies decide on that JC will have to live with?"

Meghan just laughed as she spread out the paint chips on the kitchen counter.

"The base color will be sage green," Meghan began, as she pointed to the appropriate paint sample. "The house will have white trim, and the front and back doors will be a rusty red color. What do you guys think? Not that it matters," she chuckled. "Amy and I have already made up our minds, and I ordered the paint!"

Travis put his arm around his wife's waist and gave her a kiss. "Well, of course, you have, dear. I, personally, think it will look great!"

Matt and Aiden smiled, and Matt said, "I like it. It's classy looking, and it's totally something pre-pregnant Amy would have chosen."

John picked up one of the paint samples and ran his finger over the color. "This will look nice. So, when do we start painting? I'm free anytime."

Aiden and Matt looked over to Travis and Todd, and Todd

shrugged his shoulders. "This is your project, boys," Todd said. "I'm taking some much-needed vacation time, so I'm here for the duration. You guys tell us."

Travis added, "Now that I have a very competent associate pastor, I'm taking some vacation time too. I'm all in."

Matt looked at Aiden and asked with a chuckle, "Is tomorrow too soon?"

Aiden laughed and replied, "I'm in too. Let's get it done!"

"Okay, gang," Matt said, "tomorrow morning, bright and early, we begin painting the exterior!"

* * *

Three days later, Matt and Aiden, flanked by their very dedicated crew, stood in front of the finished house. The exterior was finished and looked fantastic, just like Meghan knew it would. Bailey, Emma, and Meghan had just arrived for the final walk-through. The only people missing were JC and Amy, and they were on their way over.

JC pulled his Jeep onto the lot and parked it beside the other vehicles. Going around to the passenger side, he reached in to help a very pregnant Amy out of the Jeep.

He chuckled as he said, "I believe, dear, it's time to trade in your Honda for a newer car. Maybe an SUV with plenty of room for a car seat."

"Then we'd better make a fast trade, honey," Amy replied with a smile. "Because something tells me we'll be needing that car seat very soon."

JC helped his wife up the steps and into the house. Their hard-working entourage followed close behind. Amy stood in the middle of the living room and looked around, taking it all in. Holding her husband's hand, she slowly walked from room to room, shaking her head in disbelief.

Once the group had reassembled in the living room, Amy looked at each one with tears in her eyes. "I can't believe this. You people are so amazing. The house is beautiful. I don't know what we did to deserve this, but we are so thankful. We can never repay you for everything."

"You can tell that baby that I will always be his or her favorite uncle," Matt said with a smile. "That's all the thanks I need."

Amy replied with a laugh, "You might have to arm wrestle Jason for the title. You have a fifty-fifty chance!"

Matt walked over and hugged his sister. "Seriously, though, seeing that smile on your face is absolutely the only thanks I need. I love you, sis."

"I love you too, Matt," Amy replied.

Looking around the room once more, Amy chuckled and said, "There is no way the few pieces of furniture we have in our apartment will fill this gorgeous house. We'll have to start saving up to buy some furniture that's fit for this house."

"About that," said a voice from the corner of the room, "you already have a tab set up down at the furniture store. All you have to do is go pick out what you need."

Everyone turned toward the voice, and no one was surprised to see it belonged to none other than Mike Slater.

JC laughed and asked, "When did you sneak in, Mike? We didn't even know you were here."

"I'm sneaky like that," Mike replied with a laugh. "You all were at the other end of the house when I came in, so I just tucked myself away in the corner. Pretty clever, huh?"

Everyone laughed and surrounded Mike to dish out generous hugs and handshakes.

"Will you ever stop being so amazing, Mike?" JC asked.

Mike feigned thought for a moment as he scratched his chin,

then replied, "Nah, I don't think so. It's too much fun! Besides, I like keeping everyone guessing!"

* * *

Within a couple of days, the asphalt driveway had been poured, along with sidewalks, and the underground sprinklers had been installed. Sod was being laid, and other basic landscaping was going in. It was truly beginning to look like a finished house. JC and Amy, with the assistance of Meghan, had picked out furniture for the house, shaking their heads in disbelief whenever they decided on something and knew it was another gift from Mike. The furniture company had assured them it would all be delivered before moving day, which was coming up in a few days.

When moving day finally arrived, the family was out in full force to ensure the move was as quick and stress-free as possible for Amy. John had finished packing up the apartment, and the guys were loading their pickups with boxes. Most of their belongings were in boxes since they had very little furniture of their own in the furnished apartment. That would all stay for Bailey and Emma to use. All the clothes from the closets had been loaded into Meghan and Bailey's SUVs. Before long, the caravan of vehicles was on its way to the new house.

Throughout the flurry of activity getting things unloaded and moved into the new house, Meghan was keeping close watch over Amy. She had suggested Josh help the guys with the boxes while Bailey and Emma moved clothes into the closets. "Mama Bear" Meghan had placed herself in charge of Amy. A couple of times she noticed Amy trying to hide some discomfort, but whenever she asked, Amy insisted everything was okay. Nonetheless, Meghan alerted Josh and Travis, just in case.

Once again, Meghan looked over and noticed Amy bent over

in discomfort. She walked up to Amy and asked, "Is everything okay, Amy?"

"I'm fine," Amy insisted, as she bent over again.

Meghan took her gently by the arm and said, "Amy, dear, you're in labor."

Amy looked up at Meghan with terrified eyes. "Are you sure?"

Meghan laughed softly. "I've had three children, Amy. Yes, I'm sure."

With that, Meghan let out a shrill whistle that would have impressed any baseball coach. "Josh, get your dad and come here. Help Amy get into my SUV. We're heading to the hospital."

"The hospital?" Josh asked.

"Yes, son," Meghan said calmly. "You're about to become a father. Let's move it, everyone!"

Josh looked at his dad as they dropped everything and began running toward Meghan's car. "You heard her, son," Travis said with a chuckle. "Mama Bear has spoken. Let's get this show on the road!"

Chapter Thirteen

The hospital waiting room appeared to be hosting a family reunion. Travis, Todd, and Aiden were relaxing comfortably in the chairs along the window. Matt was pacing the floor like he was the expectant father instead of Josh. Kaci had promised the twins they could go to the hospital to await news of the baby's arrival on the condition they would sit quietly and read. Todd's wife Nicole was on duty as one of the ER nurses, so she stopped in to check on everyone periodically.

John had stopped by his house to pick up his wife Vicki, who was thrilled when Amy asked if she wanted to be in the delivery room. But Vicki was still struggling with how to fit herself back into her daughter's life, so she opted to stay in the waiting room with her husband.

Amy had given Meghan the role of surrogate mother and wanted her present in the delivery room. Since Meghan looked at Amy as another daughter, she was happy to help however Amy needed her. In the delivery room, Meghan kept most of her focus on Amy, while still trying to keep Josh calm. Amy and Josh had attended Lamaze classes, so Josh was helping Amy with her breathing. The doctor commended Amy and Josh for going with their instincts and getting right to the hospital since he expected the birth to be very soon.

"Actually," Josh told the doctor, "we can thank my mom for that. Neither of us was really expecting it for a few more days. But she knew right away that Amy was in labor."

The doctor chuckled and said, "It certainly added a little more excitement to moving day, didn't it?"

"Yes, it did!" Josh agreed.

Josh reached over and took Amy's hand in his and said, "New house and new baby all in the same day. We are certainly blessed."

Between contractions, Amy squeezed Josh's hand and replied, "God is good."

Meghan added, "All the time."

* * *

Less than an hour later, JC walked into the waiting room wearing a hospital gown over his street clothes and a huge smile. Everyone jumped up, anxious to hear his report. He looked around at his family, his heart filled with love. "It's a boy!" he reported.

Everyone swarmed around JC with hugs, handshakes, and congratulations, and they all began talking at once. John and Vicki walked up to JC and gave him a big hug, then hugged each other.

"We have a grandson, John," Vicki said with tears in her eyes.

"Yes, we do," John replied proudly.

When the nine-year-old twins were able to push their way through the crowd of grownups, they both gave their Uncle Josh a big hug.

Aaron looked up at Josh and said, "Uncle Josh since you're our uncle, does that mean the new baby will be our uncle too?"

Josh smiled and said, "No, buddy. He's your cousin."

"You mean like Aiden is our cousin?" Aaron asked, shaking his head in confusion.

"Yes, just like Aiden is your cousin," Josh replied with a smile.

"But isn't Aiden your cousin too?" Aaron asked. "How can Aiden be your cousin and my cousin, and the baby is my cousin too? He should be an uncle."

Josh just chuckled, then Aaron added, "Cousins are confusing."

Travis stepped up and patted Aaron on the shoulder. "Yes, Aaron, cousins are confusing. But having lots of cousins can sure be fun."

Turning back to Josh, Travis asked, "How's Amy, son? Can we see her and the baby?"

"She's fine, Dad," Josh replied. "The doctor wants to give her a few minutes to regroup, then you can see them. John, you and Vicki can come see them in a few minutes too. Unfortunately, everyone else will need to wait until they're released from the hospital."

Matt walked up to Josh, obviously disappointed. "What about me, JC?"

JC put his arm around the young man he considered a brother, and said with a smile, "You know, Matt, I'm pretty sure I can slip you in past the warden too. Give us a few minutes, then I'll be back."

* * *

Amy was propped up in the hospital bed with a little bundle wrapped tightly and held close to her chest. JC opened the door to her room and poked his head in.

"Are you ready for a few important visitors, honey?" JC

asked his wife.

Obviously tired, but incredibly happy, Amy smiled and replied, "Absolutely!"

JC stepped over to one side of the bed and held his wife's hand. Meghan was on the other side of the bed, all smiles. The visitors came in quietly and circled the bed.

Travis stepped up first and took a peek at his new grandson, pulling the blanket away from his face slightly. "Welcome to the world, little one. I hope you know how many people love you. You're one lucky kid."

Travis stepped back and ushered John and Vicki closer. John leaned over and kissed his daughter on the forehead while Vicki simply stared at her new grandson in disbelief.

"I promise, little guy," John whispered through tears, "I'll be a better grandpa to you than I was a dad to your mom."

Matt had been standing back patiently, waiting his turn. Once his parents stepped back a bit, he came up beside the bed, looking from his sister to his little nephew.

"He's so tiny," Matt said quietly. Then he chuckled softly, "It looks like he has your nose, sis. That's okay, though. I'm sure he'll outgrow that."

Amy smiled at her brother as she lifted her little son. "Do you want to hold him, Matt?"

"Me?" Matt asked in surprise.

"Yes, little brother, you," Amy answered with a smile. "Just make sure you support his head. Josh will show you. He's an expert already."

JC beamed with pride as he took his son from his wife and gently placed him in Matt's arms. "You're going to be an awesome uncle, Matt."

After a few minutes, it was obvious Matt was becoming nervous. "Who wants to hold him next?" he asked, looking around the room.

Travis looked over at John and said, "John, why don't you and Vicki hold your new grandson?"

Amy's parents each took a turn holding the baby, and the love on their faces for their new grandson was obvious. Amy and JC watched the bonding and knew how much that baby was going to change everyone's lives.

Eventually, John handed the baby over to Travis, who immediately began talking to the sleeping bundle.

Travis looked up at Josh and Amy and asked, "So, in the immortal words of your Uncle Todd, do you have a name for this little guy, or will we be calling him Rug Rat?"

Josh laughed and said, "Wow, that brings back memories. I had forgotten he used to call me Rug Rat."

Meghan walked around the bed to stand next to Travis as he held the baby. They both looked down at their grandson with so much love in their hearts.

Josh took Amy's hand and said, "We *have* decided on a name for him, and it's *not* Rug Rat."

Matt laughed quietly and said, "Whew, that's a good thing. I was hoping you could do better than that."

Josh smiled as he looked down at his son. "Like most new parents, Amy and I tossed around a few different names we liked but kept returning to the one we chose. This little guy's name is Levi Matthew Harmon."

Josh looked at his parents and saw tears forming in his dad's eyes.

"I hope that's okay, Dad," Josh said softly.

Travis looked at his little grandson, then looked at his son, with tears streaming down his face. "It's more than okay, son. I'm honored."

John and Vicki looked at each other in confusion. "There

obviously must be some significance to that name," John said, watching Travis.

"Yes, there is," Josh replied with tears forming in his eyes. "Years ago, before Dad and Mom met, Dad was married to a lady named Angela. She was killed by a drunk driver. She was pregnant at the time, and the baby also died in the accident. The baby was going to be named Levi."

Vicki gasped as she and John clung to each other. "Oh, my," she whispered.

Turning to Matt, JC smiled and said, "And Matthew, of course, is for you, Matt. If our son turns out to be half the man you're becoming, we couldn't ask for anything more than that."

"Wow," Matt whispered as he looked over at his little namesake. "You won't be sorry, JC, I promise."

Amy had been lying back quietly watching her family get to know her new son. "We never considered anything else for his middle name, Matt. We both love you and know you're going to be an amazing uncle to our boy."

Travis reluctantly handed Levi back to Josh, then turned to everyone and said, "We'd better let Amy rest." Turning back to Amy and Josh, he asked, "Would it be okay if we made the announcement to the gang waiting anxiously out in the waiting room?"

Amy looked at her father-in-law and said, "We were going to suggest you make the announcement. Then please tell everyone we will see them all after we're released."

* * *

Once everyone had reassembled in the waiting room, Travis looked around at his family with pride. "Josh and Amy wanted us to tell you they are looking forward to seeing everyone when they get home. They also wanted you to know their son's name is Levi Matthew Harmon."

"Hey, Uncle Matt," Sophie said, "the baby has your name!"

"Yes, he does," Matt said with pride. "He sure does."

"Dad," Kaci said, "you mentioned they will see us when they get home. Just so Josh doesn't start stressing out about things, let him know Bailey and Emma stayed at their house and got the nursery more or less set up for them. They'll probably want to change things around, but at least it will be functional for when they get home with Levi."

"Thanks, Kaci," Travis replied. "I'll be sure to let them know."

"Oh," Kaci continued, "I also called Ryleigh and she's on her way home now. She should be here in a couple of hours."

"Perfect," Travis said. "Thanks for taking care of that. Things kind of got real busy real quick."

"Aiden and I are going to head over to the house now," Todd said. "We'll make sure their bedroom is functional, so they at least have a place to crash."

"We can help too," John added. "With everyone pitching in, we should be able to make things livable for them."

"Thanks, Dad," Matt said. "Well, should we all just meet up at their house?"

As everyone hurried out of the hospital and headed to their vehicles, Travis and Meghan watched their family with pride.

"God is good," Travis said.

Meghan put her arm around her husband's waist and added, "All the time."

* * *

Everyone gathered at JC and Amy's new house and got right to work. Luckily, the furniture store had delivered the new pieces of furniture a couple of days earlier. Boxes were temporarily stashed in the proper rooms, but enough boxes were unpacked to make things livable for a few days. Both bathrooms had been set up with the basic necessities, and the kitchen was made functional. As much as everyone wanted to unpack all the boxes for JC and Amy, Kaci cautioned against that. She pointed out that this was their first house, so they were going to want to decide where to put things. In a few days, the family could offer to help with the unpacking, but it needed to be done with JC and Amy's guidance, and on their timeframe.

Meghan had escaped next door to her own home and started a big pot of spaghetti sauce and made a salad so everyone would have an easy dinner after working at Josh and Amy's.

Ryleigh arrived home amid all the chaos. It was the first time she had seen the finished house. She walked from room to room with her mom and shook her head in amazement.

"Wow, Mom," Ryleigh said. "The guys did a great job on the house. It looks amazing."

"I agree," Meghan said, nodding. "They had a lot of help, but it was their baby and they really worked hard on it."

Walking into the living room, Ryleigh looked around and asked, "So, what can I help with?"

After being introduced to Bailey and Emma, Ryleigh took an instant liking to the two girls. She got right to work helping them decorate for a welcome home party. Banners were hung in the living room showing the dual purpose of the party. Congratulations! Welcome Home! It's a Boy!

As they were hanging the banners, Ryleigh chuckled and said, "The baby was just born a few hours ago, and they didn't find out in advance it would be a boy. How did you guys manage to get an 'It's a Boy!' banner already?"

The girls chuckled before Bailey replied, pointing over at Meghan. "That would be your mom. She wanted to be prepared, so she got a girl and a boy banner a couple weeks ago."

Ryleigh laughed, "Of course she did!"

Once everyone was satisfied the house looked presentable, livable, and festive, they all walked next door for a spaghetti dinner. They were going to have a very busy day coming up.

* * *

Aaron and Sophie were the self-appointed lookouts to announce the arrival of the new baby. They had been pacing back and forth in the living room, keeping a watch out the windows.

"They're here!" Sophie yelled from the living room. "Papa and Grandma are here!"

Pointing out the living room window as people flooded into the room, Aaron said, "And there's Uncle Josh and Aunt Amy!"

"Don't just go running out there, kids," Jason said.

"But Dad," Sophie said with disappointment, "we want to see the baby."

"There will be plenty of time to see the baby," Kaci reminded her kids. "They don't need to be mobbed."

Grabbing her cousin's arm, Ryleigh said, "Come on, Aiden, let's go give them a hand."

JC had driven his mom's SUV because it was easier for Amy to get in and out of than his Jeep. He was helping his wife out of the car when she squealed in surprise.

"Ryleigh!" Amy shrieked. "I didn't know you were here!"

Ryleigh wrapped her friend in a gentle hug and said, "Where else would I be, you silly girl? My sister just had a baby. Congratulations!"

JC stepped up and gave his little sister a big hug. "This is sure a surprise. I'm so glad you made it home, Ry."

"Congratulations, JC," Ryleigh said as she took Amy by the hand and JC began following her.

"Uh," Ryleigh said, pointing to the car, "aren't you forgetting someone?"

"Oh, man!" JC said, reaching into the back seat to disconnect the baby's car seat. "This is going to take some getting used to."

Travis chuckled as he stepped up beside his son. "Do you want me to take Levi, son?"

Josh shook his head and smiled. "No, that's okay, Dad. I've got to get used to this. It's Ryleigh's fault. She took me by surprise."

"Sure," Ryleigh said as she dramatically put her hand on her heart, "always blame the little sister."

Everyone laughed as they headed toward the house. Aiden grabbed Amy's suitcase from the car and took it to their bedroom, then joined the family in the living room.

JC and Amy looked around their living room in surprise.

"Wow," Amy said. "It looks like elves have been hard at work here."

Noticing all the decorations and banners, along with a cake sitting in the middle of the dining room table, her eyes landed on a bassinet off to the side of the room.

Amy shook her head, "You guys thought of everything. Thank you all so much!"

As Ryleigh helped Amy get comfortable on the sofa, JC unbuckled his son from the car seat and gently laid him in the bassinet.

"Okay, everyone," JC said, "this is Levi. I promise you will all eventually get a chance to hold him and introduce yourselves. But he just fell asleep, so let's leave him in the bassinet for now so he can rest."

Sophie walked up to Josh and said, "Uncle Josh, can I look at him in his little bed? I promise I won't touch him. But can I see him?"

Josh knelt down and hugged his niece. "You bet, Sophie. Come on, Aaron, you can come over too."

"He's so tiny," Sophie said in amazement, as she and her brother looked over the edge of the bassinet.

Matt walked up behind them and put his hand on Sophie's shoulder. "That's exactly what I said, Sophie."

Everyone settled in for a nice long visit and took turns watching over the sleeping baby. Amy's parents were finally beginning to feel like a part of this amazing family and made a point to talk with everyone. Mike didn't seem to mind a bit when Aaron and Sophie monopolized his time. Todd and Nicole were sitting around the dining room table with Aiden, Bailey, Matt, and Emma. Aaron kept circling the cake on the table like a vulture, and Matt would wink at him and nod across the room at JC.

Aaron finally decided he couldn't stand it any longer. He looked at Matt, then looked over at Josh. "Uncle Josh, are we going to eat this cake today?"

Laughter erupted in the room as Josh looked at his nephew and chuckled, "Five minutes, buddy. Do you think you'll survive for five more minutes?"

Aaron rubbed his stomach, then smiled and said, "I think so. But not six minutes!"

Matt laughed and gave Aaron a high five. "Good job, buddy!"

Josh relaxed on the sofa next to his wife and put his arm around her, knowing full well he was going to have to get up in exactly five minutes.

He hugged his wife and said, "This is what it's all about, Amy. We have to be the luckiest people on the planet."

"Not lucky, honey," Amy replied, "blessed. So incredibly blessed."

Four and a half minutes later, Josh helped his wife up and headed toward the dining room. They had a cake to cut.

Chapter Fourteen

Somehow, with all the commotion and life changes involved in moving into a new house and having a baby, all in the same day, the family was slowly beginning to adapt to a new normal. JC and Amy had plenty of willing volunteers to help with the unpacking, including several teenagers from the youth center. Meghan had offered to help coordinate the volunteers to make sure Amy wasn't overwhelmed. JC had taken a few days off right after Levi was born, which helped immensely. Before long, their new house looked like a home.

There was a fairly constant stream of visitors stopping by to see the baby and visit with JC and Amy. With their first house completed, thus freeing up some of their time, Matt and Aiden were frequent visitors, often bringing Bailey and Emma along with them. Other family members stopped by regularly, trying to take into consideration the new mother's need for rest. Mike made a point to check in with the new parents at least once a day to see if there was anything they needed. And, of course, Aaron and Sophie checked in on their new cousin whenever they could convince someone to take them over to Uncle Josh and Aunt Amy's new house.

Ryleigh was home for a couple of weeks, and she took

advantage of spending as much time as possible with Amy and JC.

Sitting in their living room, visiting with a few family members, Ryleigh looked over at Amy and smiled. "Amy, what would you say to letting me throw you guys a housewarming party?"

"You don't have to do that, Ryleigh," Amy said in a weak protest.

"I don't have to," Ryleigh replied. "But I'd like to."

Looking across the room at Bailey and Emma, Ryleigh said, "I bet Bailey and Emma would be willing to help. It wouldn't be that hard."

"That would be so much fun!" Emma said with excitement. "Let's do it!"

Amy laughed and said, "I'm not sure when you girls would have time to plan a party. After all, you're in the middle of moving into a new apartment."

"Not a problem," Bailey replied. "There are three of us. Besides, we've already cleaned the apartment, so it's ready to move into. And our brothers have offered to pack up our things in storage and move them over from Seattle. They're going to do that this coming weekend."

"See, Amy," Emma added with a smile, "it's like we have almost nothing to do."

Meghan laughed from across the room. "I can help, and I'm pretty sure Vicki would be willing to pitch in too."

Amy smiled as she shook her head. "You guys are amazing. You've already done enough for us. But if you want to throw a housewarming party, who am I to stand in your way?"

"Hey," Emma said logically, "if you guys can have a baby and move into a new house all in the same day, we should be able to throw a little party and move into an apartment in the same week. While we're waiting for the guys to come over with the rest of our things, we can plan the party. Then we move into the apartment, which will take all of ten minutes or so, then we have the party."

Ryleigh laughed and said, "See, it's nearly planned already. And we'll have it before I head back to finish up school."

"That way maybe the boys will be able to stick around for the party and meet everyone," Bailey said. "You guys will just love them. They're computer geeks, and they're goofy, but they're very lovable."

"Sounds interesting," Ryleigh said, smiling. "I can't wait to meet them."

* * *

From the driver's seat of their borrowed pickup, Wyatt Campbell turned to his brother Spencer and asked, "Bailey said we're supposed to meet them at the apartment, right? Not at the house where they've been staying?"

"That's what she said in the text," Spencer confirmed, glancing at his phone. "She said they can get the few belongings they have at the house into their cars. She just said to text her when we get to the apartment complex, and they'll head over."

"Okay," Wyatt said. "When we get close, you can go ahead and text her."

It took the boys less than ten minutes to find the apartment complex where they pulled the pickup into an empty spot to wait for their sisters.

They didn't have to wait long. About fifteen minutes later, Spencer pointed toward the street and said, "There's Bailey now."

Once both girls parked their cars, they ran over to give their brothers hugs.

"Were you guys able to get everything from the storage unit into the truck?" Bailey asked.

"Of course," Spencer said with a satisfied chuckle. "We've played enough Tetris to figure out how to pack more belongings into a pickup than should logically fit. Speaking of which, you girls have way too much stuff."

"You only think that," Emma said as she playfully slapped her brother on the arm, "because you can survive for a month with nothing more than your laptop."

"And food," Spencer added seriously. "We have to have food."

About that time, another pickup pulled into the lot and parked beside Bailey's SUV. Two tall young men climbed out of the truck and walked toward the girls.

Bailey smiled at the two men and said, "Oh good, you got here just in time."

Turning to her brothers, Bailey introduced everyone. "Wyatt, Spencer, this is Aiden Byers and Matt Phoenix. Aiden and Matt, these are our brothers."

As Matt and Aiden shook hands with the brothers, Emma added with a laugh, "Wyatt is the older one."

Aiden walked over and put his arm around Bailey's waist. "You told us your brothers were twins," he said with a laugh. "But you didn't tell us they were identical twins. Tell us who is who so we can at least remember them by their shirt color."

Wyatt raised his hand and said as he laughed, "I'm Wyatt, the good-looking one. Today I'm modeling a stylish green shirt with a faded pair of Levis."

Next, Spencer raised his hand and added, "And I'm Spencer, the smart one. I'm wearing a Seattle Mariners t-shirt and slightly nicer Levis than my much older brother. And, by the way, it's nice meeting you guys. We've heard a lot about you."

"Uh-oh," Matt said. "Don't believe everything they've told you. Unless, of course, it was all good."

Emma smiled as she put her arm around Matt's waist. "Don't worry, Matt, it was all good stuff."

"Well," Aiden said as he started toward the loaded truck, "should we get this stuff unloaded? It shouldn't take us long."

"Bales," Wyatt said, looking at his older sister, "why don't you and Em lead the way to the apartment, and you can show us where you want things? You girls don't need to be lifting all this stuff."

Muttering under her breath about being fully capable of carrying a box, Bailey started up the stairs.

In less than an hour, the truck had been unloaded and things had been placed in the proper rooms. It took another twenty minutes to unload the clothes and a few miscellaneous items from both cars.

"We'll have to go to the grocery store at some point," Bailey said. "But for now, why don't we go back to Travis and Meghan's house? I know they want to meet you guys."

"We'll follow you guys," Spencer said, as the girls walked to Bailey's SUV. "We have their address in case we get separated."

A short time later, they pulled into the driveway at the Harmon house, where they found Travis and Meghan sitting on the front porch. The older couple stood and walked toward the driveway.

Bailey once again introduced everyone. "Travis and Meghan, we'd like you to meet our brothers, Wyatt and Spencer."

Wyatt reached out to shake Travis's hand and said with a smile, "To eliminate confusion right up front, I'm Wyatt, and I'm wearing the green shirt."

Spencer followed by shaking hands with both Travis and Meghan and said, "I'm Spencer, wearing the Mariners t-shirt."

Meghan looked at the girls with a smile and said, "Why didn't you tell us your brothers were identical twins? I could have made name tags!"

Spencer slapped his hand on his forehead and laughed. "Now, why didn't we think of that?"

"They don't need name tags, honey," Travis said to his wife, laughing. "It's easy to see that Wyatt is about six-two with dark hair, and Spencer is about six-two. With dark hair. They look nothing alike."

Wyatt laughed and said, "I think we're going to like you guys. If the rest of your family is as funny as you are, we should fit in just fine."

"Let's go around to the back deck and get comfortable," Meghan suggested as she started toward the side of the house. "Did the girls tell you about the housewarming party we're having tomorrow for Josh and Amy? I hope you'll be able to stay for it. You can meet the rest of the family."

"As luck would have it," Wyatt replied, following everyone around to the back of the house, "we both got Monday off, so we can stay through the weekend and head back to Seattle sometime Monday."

"Yeah, we came prepared," Spencer added. "We'll throw sleeping bags on the floor at the girls' apartment and crash for the weekend."

"You'll do no such thing," Meghan said in mock outrage. "We have two perfectly good bedrooms right here. It just happens they were both recently vacated by the previous guests."

Laughing, Travis looked at the boys and said, "Throw up your white flags now, boys. She won't take no for an answer."

Wyatt laughed and said, "In that case, we accept your most generous offer. I've got to warn you though, you haven't seen my brother eat."

Matt guided Emma to one of the love seats on the back deck, then sat down beside her. "It's not a problem, Wyatt. They've seen me eat, so I doubt Spencer will surprise them!"

Meghan sat down next to her husband and smiled, "I'm used to feeding growing boys. As Matt likes to say, 'I'm not complicated. Just keep me fed.' That's how most boys work. Which reminds me, Matt, why don't you go grab the tray of cookies from the kitchen counter? We have drinks in the mini fridge out here."

Matt jumped up and headed toward the kitchen, calling over his shoulder, "Meghan makes the best chocolate chip cookies! I hope she made enough!"

Emma stood and followed Matt, saying, "I'll make sure they actually make it to the deck."

After helping themselves to drinks from the mini fridge, everyone grabbed a couple cookies and settled in to get to know each other.

* * *

Everything looked great for JC and Amy's housewarming party, and the timing was perfect. Bailey and Emma had settled into their apartment, their brothers were still in town, and the party had been planned for the day before Ryleigh headed back to school. As luck would have it, the entire family would be able to attend. Even Nicole was on a four-day off cycle from the hospital.

JC and Amy were seated on the living room sofa, surrounded by gifts. With each opened gift, they shook their head in amazement at all their family had done. They received a beautiful set of dishes from Travis and Meghan, a photo album to fill with pictures of their new home from Bailey and Aiden, and a teak salad bowl set from Emma and Matt. Kaci, Jason, and the twins provided their home with a board game set that would provide hours of entertainment. Ryleigh gave them a gorgeous centerpiece for the dining room table.

Amy's mom went into the other room to bring out their unwrapped gift, a beautiful piece of wall art for their living room.

"Mom," Amy said, gazing at the landscape painting, "this is beautiful! I love it! Thank you so much."

Taking the large canvas from his wife, JC turned to her parents and said, "John and Vicki, thank you. I think the wall above the piano would be the perfect place for it."

Wyatt stood and walked toward the front door. "Come on, Spence, let's grab our gift."

JC looked at the boys in confusion. "You didn't get us a gift too, did you? You just met us a couple days ago."

"I have a feeling our sisters are becoming kind of important to you guys," Wyatt said. "So, we wanted to do our part. We didn't wrap it though."

With that, Wyatt and Spencer walked out the front door and returned a few minutes later with a box.

"A fire pit?" Amy said excitedly. "Oh, Josh, that'll be great on the back deck! I love it!"

Josh nodded his head in agreement. "What a great idea, guys. Thanks a lot!"

"Well," Todd said as he stood and started toward the back door, "as long as we're doing gifts for the outside, it's a perfect time for our gift. I'm not going to bring it inside – I think you'd both kill me if I did – but you can see it from the back deck."

Everyone headed out to the back deck where they found, sitting in the middle of the freshly sodded lawn, a new riding lawnmower.

JC ran down the steps, followed by the other guys. He climbed onto the seat of the lawnmower and grinned.

"This is awesome, Uncle Todd! And it'll make mowing this large lawn so much easier."

Standing on the back deck, Amy walked over to Todd's wife and wrapped her in a hug. "Thanks, Nicole. But you guys really shouldn't have gotten such a big gift."

Nicole chuckled and said, "I tried to talk him out of it. But you know Todd. When he gets an idea in his head, there's no changing his mind. But I have to admit, it's certainly practical."

Mike had followed the party outside and joined Amy who was now standing beside Travis and Meghan.

"I wish you would have allowed me to get you a little something for the party," Mike said with a smile.

Amy reached over and hugged Mike and replied, "No, Mike, you've already done more than enough. You supplied nearly all the furniture for our home. Thank you. Josh and I can never thank you enough for everything you have done for us. You're incredible, and I hope you know we both love you."

"I'm a lovable kind of guy," Mike replied with a chuckle. "Keep that in mind when I ask you this next question."

"Oh?" Amy asked curiously.

"Would you mind if I asked a friend to stop by?" Mike asked. "It's no one you guys know, but he's looking for someone to build a house for him. Naturally, I thought of Matt and Aiden. I haven't talked to them yet, and I will in a minute, but the guy would really like to see the first house they built. If it's okay with you, he's only about twenty minutes away. I could talk to the boys first and see if they would even be interested, then I could call him and have him stop by."

Amy looked over at Travis and Meghan and asked, "What do you think? I don't think anyone would mind."

Travis called into the backyard. "Matt, Aiden, will you guys come here for a minute?"

Running up the steps to the back deck, Matt asked, "What's up?"

"Mike wants to ask you something," Travis said.

"Now that you boys have finished building this house," Mike began, "do you think you're going to be interested in building any others? Or do you think this is a one-and-done?"

Aiden looked at Matt, then answered Mike. "Matt and I have already talked about it. Even though it was a lot of work, building this house was so rewarding. And we like the way it turned out. We absolutely want to build houses on the side."

Todd had walked up behind the boys, so he heard the conversation. "Are you guys sure? It's a lot of work."

"We're sure, Todd," Matt replied with a smile. "We've talked about it a lot. And it's not like people are going to be beating down our door every day asking us to build a house."

"Well…" Mike said with a smile, "Maybe not *every* day. But maybe today."

Matt and Aiden looked at each other in confusion. "What are you getting at, Mike?" Aiden asked.

"I have a friend who's looking for someone to build a house for him," Mike began. "I told him about you boys, and about the house you were building. He'd like to stop by to look at it. I didn't want to have him come by if you guys weren't sure you wanted to keep going."

Aiden and Matt smiled at each other, then Todd and Travis smiled as well.

"Do all those smiles mean it's a yes?" Mike asked, grinning.

"When can he stop by?" Matt asked. "And it has to be okay with Amy and JC for him to walk through their house."

"I've already asked Amy," Mike said, smiling. "He can be here in twenty minutes."

"Give him a call, Mike," Aiden said, smiling. "We'll be more than happy to give him the grand tour!"

* * *

A couple hours later, Mike was walking his friend Roger back to his pickup, flanked by Matt, Aiden, Todd, and Travis.

"Well," Roger began, "I'm very impressed by what I've seen. This is a fine house, and I predict you young men have a bright future ahead of you building houses."

"As we pointed out," Aiden reminded the man, "we both have full-time jobs. Building houses will be a side venture."

"Oh, I understand," Roger said, nodding his head. "I don't have a time frame for the house I want you to build. I'm in no hurry. I'll get together with Mike to work out some of the details, then I'll get back to you. But definitely pencil me in for house number two."

With that, Roger got into his truck and pulled out of the driveway.

Mike walked over to Matt and Aiden and put an arm around each of their shoulders. "Just so there's no confusion, you boys understand this is a paying job. He is hiring you to build a house, just like any other contractor. And he will be paying you a fair price."

"Wow," Aiden and Matt said in unison, triggering laughter from the older men.

Travis and Todd walked over and shook hands with Matt and Aiden. "I'm proud of you boys," Todd said.

"Me too," Travis added. "You said you wanted to build houses someday, and you didn't waste any time. Here you are building your dreams already."

Chapter Fifteen

Within a few short weeks, all the details had been worked out on what would become the second house built by Matt and Aiden. Mike had helped get a contract drawn up, the buyer had provided blueprints and design information, and Travis worked with the City to help the boys navigate the permitting process. The second house would be built within the city limits of Hope, in a new area being developed for residential housing.

Aiden and Matt parked their pickup along the curb where they would be building the house. Travis and Todd pulled in behind them in a Byers Construction pickup. The four men climbed out of their trucks and met on the sidewalk in front of the vacant lot.

"Well, boys," Todd said, "this looks like where house number two will be built. Mike mentioned it was in a new residential area. Nice place for a home."

"Our lives have been so busy lately that I completely missed this," Travis said with a chuckle. "I usually notice when new construction activity is going on in town."

Matt had been pacing along the sidewalk, then stopped and put his hands into the back pockets of his Levis as he stared out across the vacant lot. "Do you think this entire development is owned by Roger, the guy who hired us to build this house?"

Travis and Todd looked at each other. "You know," Travis replied, "I don't know, but I wouldn't be surprised."

"When you stop and think about it, now that we've seen where this new house will be located," Todd added, "it kind of makes sense. And we don't know anything about Roger, other than he's a friend of Mike's."

Todd walked along the sidewalk, looking at the size of the development. "What do you think, Travis?" he asked. "Based on the size of this lot, do you think this development is planning ten or twelve houses?"

"If all the lots are roughly the size of this one," Travis answered, "I'd say that's a pretty safe guess."

Aiden and Matt walked over to where Travis was pointing something out to Todd. "Wait a minute," Aiden said. "Are you saying there's a possibility that Roger may be the person planning this entire development?"

"Maybe," Todd answered.

"So, do you think he hired us to build this house," Aiden continued, "and if it goes well, he may hire us to build other houses in this development?"

"Let's not get ahead of ourselves, son," Todd cautioned. "We don't know that. But especially knowing that Roger is a friend of Mike's, I certainly wouldn't discount that as a possibility."

Matt looked at Aiden, and both young men smiled. "Aiden, we may have just gone into the house-building business without realizing it," Matt said with a huge grin.

A grinning Aiden reached out and shook Matt's hand and said, "But we won't get ahead of ourselves."

"Of course not," Matt replied chuckling. "Especially if Mike is involved in any way."

As the four men walked back to their pickups, Travis leaned

toward Todd and said with a chuckle, "I think it may be time to make a phone call to Mike Slater."

* * *

Travis and Meghan were relaxing on the back deck of their home, waiting for Todd and Nicole to arrive. After a recent phone call with Mike, they decided the time was right to make some changes.

Meghan heard a pickup pull up out front and texted her brother that they were around back. Within a couple of minutes, Todd and Nicole walked into the side yard and joined them on the deck.

"Hi, Nicole," Meghan greeted her sister-in-law. "I bet it's nice having a few days off."

"You know it!" Nicole replied.

Not one to beat around the bush, Todd sat in one of the patio chairs and said, "That was an interesting phone call with Mike, wasn't it?"

"It sure was," Travis replied. "It's nice to have confirmation of our suspicions. So, Roger *is* the one planning that housing development."

"We all knew the boys wanted to try building houses on the side," Todd said. "It turns out they're pretty good at it. And I'm not sure how they managed, but they got that first house built and still worked more than full-time at the construction company."

"Ah," Meghan said, "to be young again and have that kind of energy!"

Travis laughed and said, "I shudder when I think of all the ways I spread myself thin when I was their age!"

"We've discussed this idea a few times," Meghan began, "and it seems like the time is right. The boys have proven themselves with their first house. They already have a contract to build a second one. It's time we made it official."

"Agreed, sis," Todd said, nodding. "It's time to create a home-building arm for Byers Construction. It won't be a separate company. Instead, it will be part of the construction company. I think it's important to both the boys, especially Matt, to have something they can call their own. When I discussed it with Aiden the other night, he felt pretty strongly about having Matt's name on the business in some way. He has a lot of respect for Matt and for the struggles he's overcome to get to where he is now. I agree with Aiden."

"I think that's a wonderful idea, Todd," Meghan said in agreement. "Did Aiden have any ideas on what to call the home-building portion of the company?"

"Actually," Todd said with a smile, "he had what I thought was a great idea. What do you guys think of calling it Phoenix Rising Homes?"

Travis, Meghan, and Nicole looked at each other, then back to Todd. They all smiled.

"I love it!" Nicole said with enthusiasm.

"I think it's perfect," Travis said, nodding.

Nodding her head, Meghan said, "Phoenix Rising Homes, a subsidiary of Byers Construction. It has a nice ring to it."

"I think we should get business cards printed up for the boys," Travis suggested. "Then schedule a meeting with them."

After discussing some of the business details a bit further, discussions turned to the house next door, where the newest member of the family had quietly wormed his way into everyone's heart.

* * *

If Matt and Aiden thought they'd been busy before, that was

nothing compared to how busy they were about to become. With a contract in hand to build the second house, and the prime weather for construction projects beginning to wane, they knew they had a big job ahead of them. They would have to get the house built and the exterior nearly finished before winter. Then they could work on finishing the interior of the house once the weather turned colder and wetter.

The two young men learned a lot during the construction of their first house. They quickly learned they weren't able to do *all* the actual work themselves, especially while holding down a full-time job at Byers Construction. Under the tutelage of both Travis and Todd, they quickly learned the value of subcontractors. They had been discussing that topic when Todd, Meghan, and Travis joined them in the office of Byers Construction for a meeting.

Walking into the office and closing the door, Todd turned to Aiden and asked, "Do you have someone manning the front counter for you while we have this meeting?"

"Yeah," Aiden replied. "Steve has it covered. He can handle anything that comes up. That way we won't be interrupted."

Todd smiled. "Good choice. Steve's a good man."

The small group took seats around the conference table, and Meghan set a small box beside her on the table.

"Well, guys," Todd addressed the younger men with a smile, "has life gotten busy enough for you?"

"It's definitely busy," Matt replied, "but I love it! It's great!"

"I agree," Aiden said, nodding. "There sure hasn't been time to get bored."

"Well," Todd said, "let's get down to business. You now have the footings on the house finished and all the subfloors have been laid. So, you're ready to begin framing. It's going into fall now, so we'll start running out of good weather for building. You've got to get the house constructed and most, if not all, of the exterior finished before bad weather hits. Then you can work on the interior when weather prevents outside work."

The young men nodded in understanding.

"The only way that's going to happen," Todd continued, "is if we hire some more laborers. Once some of the commercial projects slow down, a lot of those guys can be pulled away to help with the house construction. But I still think we're going to need more workers, especially at the beginning."

"I agree," Aiden said. "The sooner we hire more help, the faster we can get the house up."

"Matt," Todd said, "do you think your dad would be interested in a permanent full-time job? He certainly proved himself on JC and Amy's house. He learned a lot and seemed to enjoy the work."

"I think he'd love the idea," Matt replied. "He was just telling me again the other day how much he likes doing the construction work."

"Okay," Todd said. "Why don't you guys hire John as a permanent employee, then we can all get busy finding additional laborers."

"As you guys are aware," Travis spoke up, "the three of us are working toward retirement, so we're slowly easing into part-time work. One advantage of that is that it frees us up to help with the house-building projects."

Both young men nodded, and Matt said, "I hope you know how much Aiden and I appreciate all the work you've all done. And I don't mean just physical labor. I mean everything you've taught us about subcontractors, the permit process, and everything else. There's no way we could do this without your experience and willingness to mentor us. So, thanks."

"It's been our pleasure," Meghan said with a smile. "It's kind of nice to pass along some of our experience to such willing students. You guys have certainly made us proud."

"Travis, Meghan, Nicole, and I got together for a meeting a few days ago," Todd began. "You boys proved yourselves on the house for JC and Amy, and you've been hired to build a second house. So, we decided it was time to make a little change. Byers Construction is going to officially branch out into residential construction as Phoenix Rising Homes, a subsidiary of Byers Construction. What do you think?"

Matt could have been knocked over with a feather. "Wow," he said quietly. "But wait a minute. Aiden and I have been doing this together. His name should be in there too, not just mine."

"Actually, Matt," Todd explained, "the name Phoenix Rising Homes was Aiden's idea."

Matt turned to Aiden and asked, "But why?"

"Matt," Aiden said, "you're like the little brother I never had. I have so much respect for you and everything you've been through. You've worked hard for this, and I think you deserve something you can call your own." Then Aiden added with a smile, "Besides, my name is already on Byers Construction."

"Wow," Matt said quietly. "You guys are the best. I promise to make you proud."

"You already have, Matt," Todd said. "You already have."

Then Meghan reached over and opened the small box she had brought in at the beginning of the meeting. Inside the box were two smaller boxes. She handed one box to Travis, and the other to Todd.

"Since you boys are officially building houses now," Travis began, "it only seems fitting that you should have business cards."

Travis handed a box to Matt while Todd handed the second box to Aiden.

Both young men opened their boxes simultaneously and took out a business card.

Aiden began reading his card. "Phoenix Rising Homes, a subsidiary of Byers Construction." Aiden grinned, then continued reading. "Aiden Byers, General Contractor."

Matt looked at his card, showed it to Aiden, and said, "Look, mine says the same thing. Only it says Matthew Phoenix, General Contractor. That is so cool!"

They all stood and shook hands. Matt walked around the table and gave everyone a hug.

Aiden and Matt both wore big grins on their faces. They hugged each other, then Matt stepped back and puffed out his chest theatrically. "We're general contractors now, Aiden. How cool is that?"

"That is very cool, Matt," Aiden replied. "Very cool, indeed!"

* * *

Matt parked his pickup along the curb in front of his parent's house and ran up the sidewalk to the front door. He burst through the door and looked around the room until he saw his dad sitting at the dining room table drinking a cup of coffee.

John looked at his son and laughed. "No more knocking when you arrive, huh, son? You don't know how good that makes me feel."

Matt could hardly contain his excitement, having just left the Byers Construction office. "Look, Dad," he said, handing his dad one of his new business cards.

John took the card in his hand and began to read, "Phoenix Rising Homes, a subsidiary of Byers Construction. Matthew Phoenix, General Contractor. Is this for real, son?"

"Yes," Matt said proudly. "It sure is! Aiden and I are officially in the house-building business! Which brings me to the reason for my visit. How would you like to be a permanent, full-time employee of Phoenix Rising Homes?"

"Are you serious, Matt?" John asked.

"Absolutely serious, Dad," Matt replied with a smile. "We need to hire some additional workers to help build houses. We just got started on the second one. What do you say? Do you want to come to work with us and build houses?"

"You probably need to run that by Todd," John replied.

"Todd is the one who suggested it," Matt said.

"Really?" John asked in surprise. "Todd suggested you hire me?"

"Yep," Matt replied. "What do you say, Dad? I know you really enjoyed working on JC and Amy's house. We need workers. We're going to be in a time crunch on this second house. We've got to get the house up and the exterior finished before bad weather hits."

John had been quietly sipping his coffee, but now he set his cup down and gave Matt his undivided attention. The grin on his face grew wider before he said, "I'd love to, son. Working alongside my son building houses. That's a very different life than I had a few years ago."

Matt reached out and put his hand on his dad's arm. "That life is dead and gone, Dad. It's time for a new life. So, are you in?"

"You can count me in, son!" John replied enthusiastically. "Thank you. And be sure to thank Todd for me. What is it Travis always says? God is good?"

"Yep," Matt confirmed. "God is good. All the time."

* * *

Two Byers Construction pickups pulled onto the lot where they would start the framing on the second house. Todd and Travis climbed out of one truck, and Aiden and Matt climbed out of the other. The four men grabbed their tool belts and hard hats and began setting up tools and sawhorses on the subfloors so they could get to work. Lumber had already been delivered earlier in the morning, and their crew would be arriving shortly.

As he was setting up a sawhorse, Matt pointed to a large sign that had been erected in the development a short distance away. "Hey, what's that?"

"That's new," Todd said as the four walked toward the large sign.

"Coming Next Year," Aiden began reading. "Hope Estates. R & M Development. I guess that makes the development official."

"R & M Development," Travis said, rubbing his chin. "Roger?"

"And Mike?" Todd asked. "It could be rather interesting."

"Maybe Roger's wife is Mary," Travis proposed with a smile.

"And maybe not," Todd added with a chuckle. "R & M Development. Go figure."

Chapter Sixteen

After taking some time off after Levi's birth, Amy returned to work at the youth center. The timing couldn't have been better. School was about to start back up after the summer break, so JC's Hope would get busy in the afternoons. When Amy first began helping out at the center not long after it opened, she quickly found her calling was tutoring the high school kids who frequented the center. She enjoyed working with the teenagers and sharing their victories when their test scores improved.

A nice perk of her and Josh owning JC's Hope was that she was able to take baby Levi to work with her. She had set up a portable playpen in the corner of the office, and it wasn't long before many of the teenagers made a point to stop in to see Levi every day. It also made it easy for Mike to see Levi regularly since he stopped by the center several times a week. Amy soon discovered that she was seeing her mom a lot more too, because Vicki dropped by to check on her grandson at least twice a week.

Amy was sitting on the sofa in the office, feeding Levi his bottle, when there was a soft knock at the door. She looked up to see her mom standing in the doorway wearing a smile.

"Are you busy, Amy?" Vicki asked. "Is it okay if I come in and visit for a bit?"

"Of course, Mom," Amy replied with a smile. "Josh and I have told you before, you're welcome to stop by anytime. Come on over and have a seat."

Vicki sat down beside her daughter and looked over at her grandson.

"Would you like to feed Levi his bottle, Mom?" Amy asked.

"I'd love to, if you don't mind."

Amy handed her son and his bottle over to her mom and watched them get settled in. Vicki immediately began singing a soft lullaby to her grandson. It wasn't long before Levi was fast asleep.

Still holding her grandson in her arms, Vicki looked over at her daughter. "You know, Amy," she began, "I have so much to apologize to you for."

Sensing her mother's need to talk, Amy didn't interrupt.

"I have so many regrets," Vicki continued, her eyes tearing up a bit. "I wasn't the mother you or Matt needed. I'm sure by now you've done the math, but I was only sixteen when you were born. Your dad was barely seventeen. Not much older than most of the kids who come here to the center. We were too young to be parents. We had no idea what we were doing. It was easier to go out partying with our friends. I was never there for you when you needed me, Amy, and I'm so sorry for that. I look at this precious little boy of yours and think about how lucky he is to have two parents who love him and want nothing but the best for him.

"This youth center that you and JC are running," Vicki continued, "it's a wonderful thing you two are doing. If it weren't for this center, a lot of these kids would probably end up like your dad and I, making a mess of our lives. But these kids have hope. And they have a support system to help them succeed. I wish there had been something like this around when your dad and I were teenagers. Maybe we wouldn't have made such a mess of things.

"I would sure like to try to make things up to you and Matt," Vicki said quietly, looking down at the sleeping baby in her arms. "I know you kids don't need a mom and dad anymore, but I'd sure like to be able to be a good grandma to Levi."

Amy reached over and put her hand on her mother's arm. "Mom," Amy said quietly, "I will always need my mom. And my dad. And I know Matt feels the same way. Neither of you are the same person you were a few years ago. You've buried that life. Let it go so you can move on. Don't keep living in the past." Then Amy added with a chuckle, "There's no future in the past, Mom."

Vicki looked up at her daughter and smiled. "You've turned into a remarkable young woman, Amy. You know your dad is going to work full-time for Matt and Aiden, don't you?"

"Yes," Amy replied, "Matt told me. I think that's great. He really seems to like the construction work."

"I need to start looking for a job now too," Vicki said. "I need something to do so I feel like I'm making a difference, even if it's something small."

"Mom," Amy said suddenly, "why don't you come to work here at the center?"

"Here?" Vicki asked in surprise. "What would I ever do here that would be helpful to anyone?"

"Are you kidding, Mom?" Amy said. "There is always work to be done around here, and it seems like we never have enough hands. When I first started helping out here, I did a lot of cleaning and tidying. Keeping the kitchen clean and the classrooms and gym tidy. It's not glamorous work, but it's necessary and it's helpful. I could talk to Josh and see what he says, but I know we could use the help. Would you be interested?"

"Sure!" Vicki answered. "I don't need to have glamorous work. I just need to know that whatever I'm doing is helping in some way. Talk it over with Josh, and you can let me know. Now

I'd better get out of here so you can get some work done."

The two women stood and embraced in a hug. Vicki smiled at her daughter and said, "When Levi wakes up, tell him Grandma Vicki stopped by to see him. And tell him I love him very much."

"I will, Mom," Amy said as her mother walked out the door.

She's going to be alright, Amy thought to herself. *Mom and Dad are both going to be alright. God is so good.*

* * *

Watching the leaves on the trees begin to change color as summer came to an end had been one of Meghan's favorite pastimes ever since she was a little girl. She was so relaxed, sitting on the back deck marveling over the colorful trees in their yard, that she didn't hear anyone approach. She turned to look behind her after hearing a soft chuckle.

"Yep," Travis said to Todd and Nicole. "Meghan is off in her own little world. That happens a lot this time of year."

Travis leaned over and kissed his wife on the cheek, then sat down beside her on the loveseat. Todd and Nicole smiled as they sat down on the other loveseat.

"She always was a dreamer," Todd said with a smile. Then he quickly added, "Not that there's anything wrong with that!"

"I want it noted," Meghan said, smiling, "dreamer or not, I was the first one to this meeting."

"True, sis," Todd replied with a chuckle. "We'll give you that. One of these days maybe we'll run out of reasons to have these family meetings. So, should we get on with it? Since we've all started stepping back from our responsibilities to ease into retirement, we need to get the long-range plan for the business nailed down."

"As we said we would do," Meghan began, "Travis and I

talked to Josh and Ryleigh before mentioning any of this to the others. Mostly because we were pretty sure what they would say. And we were right. They both said it wouldn't be fair to give them a percentage of the company because neither of them has really been involved in it. They both also mentioned that Kaci and Aiden have always been the ones who stayed connected with the business, and they were the ones who stepped up to begin taking over some of the duties and responsibilities. Josh and Ryleigh both want whatever percentage they might get to be divided between Aiden and Kaci."

"They're good kids," Todd said in admiration. "Not many young adults would be that mature. But they *are* family, and they still deserve to have a share of the company."

Todd pulled out the spiral notebook they had been using for several recent meetings. "Okay, let's go over the figures we discussed last time, and see if we're all still in agreement. Since we now have the house-building branch of the business, that's going to boost the bottom line of the company as a whole. That will make all these percentages more lucrative, so to speak. Based on our last discussion, it was decided that Nicole and I would retain twenty-five percent ownership of Byers Construction and its subsidiary, Phoenix Rising Homes. Meghan, you and Travis would also retain twenty-five percent ownership. Kaci, Aiden, and Matt will each be given fifteen percent ownership of the company. That totals ninety-five percent. Even though JC and Ryleigh don't feel they deserve any interest in the company, they're both part of the next generation, and this company is part of their legacy. I think we need to give each of them half of the remaining five percent.

"And I want to make sure everyone is on the same page when it comes to Matt," Todd added. "I know I'm the one who suggested he be given ownership shares equal to Kaci and Aiden, but I want to make sure everyone is okay with that. It's not just my company."

"Meghan and I have discussed it, Todd," Travis said. "We agree with you one hundred percent. Matt has proven himself over and over from the time he was an apprentice in high school. He deserves to have a share of the company. And we wouldn't even have a residential construction branch if he hadn't wanted to build homes. He deserves it, and we want him to have equal shares with Kaci and Aiden."

"Okay," Todd said, nodding his head. "It sounds like it's time to schedule another family meeting with the kids. We need to tell them our retirement plans, and the plans to transfer ownership of the company. We may as well tell them about dividing up that five acres as well. Put all our cards on the table."

Turning to Meghan, Todd continued, "I know Ryleigh is almost finished with her master's degree, then she'll be coming home – at least for a while. Do you think we need her here in person for this meeting? Or do you think it would work for her to phone in?"

"I honestly think she would be just fine with joining by phone," Meghan replied. "We can answer whatever questions she might have. I think that would be better than interrupting her studies again for another trip home when she's so close to finishing."

"Okay," Todd agreed. "Why don't you give her a call in the next few days and see what her schedule is? Then we'll plan the meeting with the other kids around Ryleigh's schedule. And now, sis, you can sit back and enjoy this early fall weather."

* * *

Less than a week later, another family meeting was scheduled at

Travis and Meghan's house. Todd and Nicole had arrived half an hour before the scheduled meeting time and were sitting around the dining room table visiting with Travis and Meghan. The others should begin arriving shortly. Aiden was planning to pick up Matt, and JC and Amy would be coming directly from the youth center as soon as JC finished a meeting. Jason and Kaci were dropping the kids off at the sitter after he got off work.

"I brought the notebook with our notes," Todd said as he laid the spiral notebook on the table. "Do we need anything else? I couldn't think of anything."

"No," Meghan answered, "I think that should give us everything we need for the meeting. And I'm sure we can answer whatever questions may come up."

About that time the front door opened, and JC and Amy walked into the living room carrying Levi, followed by Aiden and Matt. The four young adults joined the others in the dining room.

"You guys are beginning to make a habit of having these family meetings," Josh said with a chuckle as he handed Levi to his mom.

"You've never liked family meetings, son," Travis said, laughing. "That was why everyone was so surprised when you actually scheduled a meeting when you and Amy got engaged. We knew if *you* requested one, it had to be important!"

The front door opened once again, and Kaci and Jason walked in and joined the others around the dining room table. "Sorry we're late," Jason apologized. "My meeting ran a little longer than anticipated."

"No problem, Jason," Todd said. "Okay, it looks like we have everyone. Meghan, do you want to go ahead and get Ryleigh on the phone?"

"Hey, everybody," Ryleigh said once her call was put on speakerphone.

"Glad you could join us, Ryleigh," Todd said. "Okay, shall we get started? I know how much everyone just *loves* these family meetings, so we'll try to make it relatively painless."

As the group chuckled, Todd continued, "You all know that us old folks are trying to ease into retirement, so we've been cutting back to part-time as much as possible. That means we've been discussing some changes that need to happen so we can eventually retire. As you all know, Dad founded Byers Construction many years ago with not much more than a dream. He built it into a respected and profitable company. Earning respect was a lot more important than being profitable to Dad, but he managed to do both. Meghan and I took over the company after Dad passed away and have tried to maintain his values and ethics in the way we do business and treat our customers. The company has grown beyond Dad's wildest expectations, and we've recently added a branch of the company dedicated to building houses. So, we decided the time was right to prepare the company for its third generation."

Meghan added, "Kaci has already taken over most of my responsibilities for running the business end of the company. And Aiden has moved into handling a lot of Todd's responsibilities for the day-to-day operations. That's allowed both of us to step back a bit, and we want to thank you for your willingness to take the reins."

"We'll be getting all these changes made through the attorneys to make everyone's lives easier," Todd continued. "Moving forward, Nicole and I will retain twenty-five percent ownership of Byers Construction and its subsidiary, Phoenix Rising Homes. Meghan and Travis will also retain twenty-five percent. The remaining fifty percent ownership will be divided as follows: Kaci, Aiden, and Matt will be given fifteen percent each. JC and Ryleigh will each be given two-and-a-half percent ownership in the company.

"Let me answer some of the questions I see on your faces before you need to ask," Todd continued. "JC and Ryleigh insisted they shouldn't receive any ownership interest because they've never really been involved in the company. We've discussed it and decided we still want them to have part of the company because it's their legacy too, and Dad would have wanted it that way. So, two-and-a-half percent to each of you."

Todd looked across the table and met the eyes of a very confused Matt.

"Then there's Matt," Todd said with a smile.

Kaci jumped in before Todd could go any further. "Uncle Todd," Kaci began, "you don't need to explain Matt. We all consider him part of the family, and he deserves part ownership. I, for one, am thrilled you guys have decided to include him."

"Wow," Matt said quietly. "I don't know what to say. You guys are unbelievable. You taught me that it was okay for me to have dreams. And every single day you're helping my dreams come true. I love you guys."

Travis and Todd reached across the table to shake Matt's hand, and Aiden smiled and patted him on the back.

"We have one other item to discuss," Todd said. "Then we can move on to something more fun, like eating pizza. Luigi's should be here any minute with dinner.

"When Aiden and Matt began talking about building a house for JC and Amy," Todd continued, "we bought that five-acre parcel next door. Not long after purchasing it, we did a short plat to divide it into four parcels. Each parcel is one and a quarter acres. JC and Amy's house sits on one of those four parcels. The remaining three parcels will go to Aiden, Ryleigh, and Matt. Kaci already told us she and her family want to stay right where they are in town, so she has no interest in any of that land. We'll get the other parcels staked out and the three of you can decide among yourselves who gets which one. Then we'll make sure ownership is transferred over to you. The land will be yours to do with as you please. You can build a house of your own, or you can sell it. We obviously would prefer the lots stay in the family, but that's not a requirement."

Todd looked around the room just as the doorbell rang, then asked, "Does anyone have any questions? Or are we ready to eat some pizza?"

Ryleigh spoke up on the phone, "First of all, I want to make sure Amy gets my share of the pizza since I'm not there! Secondly, I want you all to know how glad I am to be part of this family. I love the way decisions are always made to serve the best interests of everyone in the family. I love you all. Now, I have to go, and you guys need to answer the door and get that yummy pizza!"

With that, Matt and Aiden both jumped up to answer the doorbell.

Chapter Seventeen

Fall was in the air, and the early mornings had a bit of a nip to them. The leaves on the trees were showing off their beautiful autumn colors before they would drop to the ground in a few weeks. Matt and Aiden had hired several more laborers to help on the house, so construction was moving along quickly. They also made sure to carve out time to spend with Bailey and Emma.

Emma wanted to squeeze in as much time as possible at the batting cages before they shut down for the season, so she and Matt tried to hit the cages a couple times a week. Bailey had fallen in love with the community park and couldn't get enough of the trees with their colorful leaves. When she discovered a gazebo at the park that she hadn't been aware of, it quickly became her favorite place to hang out.

Aiden parked his pickup next to Bailey's SUV at the park, grabbed the cooler from the passenger seat, and walked over to meet Bailey. As she climbed out of her car, she reached up and gave Aiden a kiss.

"Mmm," Aiden said with a smile. "I could get used to that."

Bailey smiled and took his hand, then they walked toward the gazebo.

As they emptied the contents of the cooler onto the picnic

table, Bailey walked over and leaned against the gazebo railing. "I can't believe I didn't know this gazebo was here. I could sit here for hours and simply take in the scenery. It's so beautiful."

"Although it's a different kind of beauty," Aiden began, "you should see the park and the gazebo during the winter when there's snow on the ground and they have the gazebo lit up. It's really something."

"Oh, I can imagine!" Bailey replied. "How did I ever miss this?"

"We usually come into the park from the other side," Aiden explained. "I guess I never thought about not being able to see it from that side. I've always known it was here, so it didn't occur to me that you hadn't seen it."

Bailey began looking through the things on the table. "So, what did you bring us for lunch today?"

"Aunt Meghan sent some leftover roast beef home with me last night," Aiden replied as he opened a container. "So, I made roast beef sandwiches. Then I just tossed in some chips, cookies, and a couple bottles of water."

"Sounds great!"

Aiden sat down beside Bailey at the picnic table where they ate in silence for a few minutes.

"Are you going to be working on the house this afternoon, Aiden?"

"Yeah," he replied. "It's been nice having more workers on this house. It frees up some of our time. And the commercial projects are beginning to slow down now, so we've been able to put some of those guys to work on the house. It's kind of a win-win situation. They don't have to be laid off for the winter, and it means we can keep making headway on the house."

"Do you think you'll be able to get the outside of the house done before the bad weather hits?" Bailey asked.

"I think so," Aiden replied. "I know Roger said he didn't really have a time frame to complete this house, but we don't want to drag it out. If there's a possibility that he may hire us to build some of the other houses in the development, we want to be able to prove we can get it done in a reasonable amount of time."

"You know," Bailey began, "you and Matt are sure turning some heads. Travis was telling me the other day how impressed he and Todd are with not only the quality of work you two are doing, but also with your work ethics. You guys have been working hard on these houses."

"The nice thing is that we're also having fun," Aiden said. "Matt and I work well together. I can't believe what a natural he is."

"Do you think you'll be hired to build other houses for Roger?"

"I don't know," Aiden replied. "I hope so. It would sure jumpstart the business if we were able to say we built several of the houses in that development."

Once they both finished eating, Aiden stood and began gathering things to put back into the cooler. Then he took Bailey's hand to help her up. He pulled her into his arms and said, "You need to get back to work, and I have to get over to the job site."

Bailey looked up into his eyes and sighed, "I know."

They shared a brief kiss before walking back to the parking lot, hand in hand.

Before helping Bailey into her SUV, Aiden leaned over and gave her another tender kiss. "Thanks for joining me for lunch, Bailey."

"Anytime," she replied. "Have a good afternoon."

Aiden watched her drive out of the parking lot and silently thanked God for bringing that wonderful woman back into his life.

* * *

Aiden pulled his pickup onto the lot and parked next to Matt's truck. The crew had been hard at work all morning putting plywood up for the exterior walls and the roof. Before long, they would be able to wrap the house with the vapor barrier and begin roofing. Construction was going much faster than on the first house, where Matt and Aiden were doing the lion's share of the work.

Matt called to Aiden from the roof as he started climbing down the ladder. Reaching the ground, he reached out and shook Aiden's hand.

"I wanted to let you know the roofing shingles are going to be delivered this afternoon," Matt began. "We should be finished with the plywood on the roof before the shingles arrive. Do you think we should pull a couple guys off the walls to help start laying shingles? Or would that be too many people on the roof, and they would just get in each other's way?"

"Dad said he was going to stop by to help this afternoon as well," Aiden said. "He likes doing the shingles, and he's pretty fast. I vote we see if he wants to work one side of the roof, then maybe have two other guys working the opposite side."

"That's a good idea," Matt said in agreement. "That way, maybe we can finish sheeting the walls this afternoon and be ready for the vapor barrier and maybe even some windows tomorrow.

"Did you and Bailey have a good lunch?" Matt asked.

Aiden smiled before replying. "Yeah, it was nice and relaxing. She sure likes going to the park."

Matt nodded in understanding just as Todd pulled up along the curb in his Byers Construction truck.

Work continued on the house throughout the afternoon. By the time the crew called it quits for the day, the weather was cooling quickly, and the sun was beginning to drop.

As they began to gather tools, Matt walked up to Todd and Aiden. "Do you guys mind if I cut out a few minutes early? I promised Emma I would try to meet her at the batting cages for a little bit before it gets too dark to see."

"Go for it," Aiden said.

"You've been here since early this morning, Matt," Todd said in agreement. "Go on. We'll finish up here. Tell Emma I said hi."

"Thanks!" Matt shouted over his shoulder as he removed his hard hat and sprinted to his pickup. "See you later!"

* * *

Matt parked next to Emma's Honda and jogged over to the batting cages. Emma was already practicing, and Matt smiled when he noticed she had it set for baseballs instead of softballs. She was getting some pretty decent hits, too. He stepped into the cage behind her and waited for her to swing at the next pitch.

"I'm impressed," Matt said, shutting off the pitching machine.

Emma walked over and kissed Matt, then offered him the baseball bat.

"Your turn," she said with a grin. "See if you can figure out the timing for softball."

Holding up a bat, he said, "I'll use my own bat. I've got it trained.

"I have to admit, Emma," Matt said with pride, "you've been working hard to get the timing down on the baseballs. You could be working on fine-tuning your softball skills, but instead, you're tackling baseballs. I'm really proud of you. I saw some of those hits, and they were pretty impressive."

Emma gently pushed Matt toward the batter's box and switched the pitching machine to softball.

"Show me what you've got, shortstop," Emma said with a smile.

Since he was more used to the faster pitches in baseball, it took Matt a couple of pitches before he was able to connect with the larger softballs. Once he got into the rhythm, he hit every pitch. He and Emma took turns batting, switching between baseball and softball. They finally called it quits when the lights surrounding the batting cages switched off for the night. Grabbing their bats, they walked toward the parking lot, hand in hand.

"Does Hope have any summer softball leagues?" Emma asked as they got to their vehicles.

"Yeah, we do," Matt replied, smiling. "With the AAA team here in town, baseball and softball are pretty big deals. We have men's leagues, women's leagues, and even co-ed leagues. Do you think you might be interested in joining a softball team next year?"

"I would love to!" Emma said with excitement. "You know, I played varsity softball in high school, and I played in college, too."

"You did?" Matt asked in surprise. "You never told me that before."

Emma smiled and said, "You never asked. I'm pretty good, you know."

"I wouldn't be a bit surprised," Matt laughed. "Are you interested in joining a women's league or the co-ed league?"

"I think I'll check into both of them," Emma replied. "That would be a lot of fun. You should join too, Matt. Wouldn't that be great if we could be on the same co-ed team?"

"That would be a lot of fun," Matt agreed. "It would depend

on how busy we get building houses, though. I'd hate to commit to being on a league, then have to bail a lot of the time. So, I'll have to see how things look in the spring when it's time to sign up for leagues."

Emma put her baseball bat into the back seat of her car, then turned and pulled Matt into a hug.

He leaned down and gave her a tender kiss, never releasing her from his arms. "What are you going to do now? If you don't have plans, do you want to go over to Luigi's with me? I'm hungry for pizza."

Emma laughed and said, "You're always hungry, Matt."

"True," he agreed, laughing. "But right now, I'm very specifically hungry for pizza."

"Sounds good to me," Emma said. "I'll meet you over there."

When they pulled into Luigi's parking lot a few minutes later and started walking toward the building, Matt pointed across the lot and asked, "Isn't that Bailey's SUV over there?"

Emma looked in the direction he was pointing and replied, "Yeah, I think it is."

As soon as they walked into the building, they saw Bailey and Aiden waiting to be seated.

"Hey," Emma said, as she walked up to her sister. "I didn't know you guys were coming here for dinner."

"I didn't either," Bailey laughed in reply. "It was kind of a last-minute decision."

"Us too," Matt said.

About that time, the hostess came over to seat them. "How many?" she asked.

"Why don't you guys join us?" Aiden suggested. Turning to the hostess, he answered, "There will be four of us."

As they walked to their table, Emma said, "This is kind of nice. It's been a while since the four of us have gone out to dinner together."

Matt laughed and said, "I'm not sure how together it is. I know for a fact we brought at least three different vehicles because we saw Bailey's car out there."

"Make that four," Aiden added with a laugh. "I met Bailey here too."

Everyone laughed as the guys pulled out the girls' chairs and they settled in to enjoy pizza and friendship.

Chapter Eighteen

With more men on the job, the exterior construction of the house was progressing faster than expected. Even so, Matt and Aiden had been spending many hours working on the house, in addition to keeping things running at the construction company. Work shifted from the house to commercial projects as their crews finished up a couple smaller jobs before winter. The house project was at a temporary standstill while waiting for a delayed siding delivery.

Matt walked into the break room at Byers Construction and stood in front of the vending machine. After considering his options, he dropped in some coins and punched the buttons to buy a bag of chips and a candy bar. Then he dropped some coins into the other vending machine and got a can of soda. He turned to sit on the sofa and saw Aiden sitting at one end, with his head tipped back and his eyes closed.

As Matt sat down on the other end of the sofa, Aiden opened his eyes and said, "That looks like a nutritious lunch."

"I hope I didn't wake you," Matt apologized. "I didn't notice you sitting there when I came in."

"No problem," Aiden said as he sat up. "I wasn't napping, just thinking."

"It's kind of nice to have a little break, isn't it?" Matt said.

"Yeah," Aiden agreed. "It's fun working on the house, but it does get exhausting."

"At least we have actual crews helping out on *this* house," Matt commented. "That first house was brutal."

"That's a fact," Aiden nodded in agreement. "Your dad's been a big help too. Before long, he could probably be made a crew foreman, if we get more houses to build and stay busy."

"I think he would like that. He's taking this job seriously," Matt added.

"So, were you thinking about anything important?" asked Matt.

"Huh?"

"You said you weren't napping, you were thinking," Matt said.

"Oh, yeah," Aiden laughed. "Actually, it is pretty important."

"Anything you want to talk about?" Matt asked.

Aiden turned on the sofa, so he was facing Matt. "Bailey and I have been spending a lot of time together. Well, as much time as work will allow."

"Yeah, I know," Matt said. "It's been hard to find time to spend with the girls, but somehow we've managed."

"You know Bailey and I knew each other from our time in the Army, right?" Aiden asked.

"I remember," Matt said, smiling.

Aiden stared off into space but had a smile on his face. Seemingly talking to no one in particular, he said, "She's pretty special. She has such a good and kind heart. It's no surprise she went into the ministry."

"She's a natural for pastoring, that's for sure," Matt agreed. "I really enjoy her sermons at church."

No longer staring off into space, Aiden looked at Matt and

said, "I'm going to ask Bailey to marry me."

Matt jumped off the sofa, reached for Aiden's hand, and pulled him up into a hug. "Wow, Aiden! That's fantastic! When did you decide that?"

"Last night," Aiden answered. "I've been thinking about it a lot. Since she moved here, we've really reconnected. Not having to worry about Army regulations or what people may think, it's been nice to just be ourselves. We've been able to relax and enjoy each other's company."

"She'll be getting a great guy, Aiden," Matt said sincerely. "I mean that. She couldn't ask for anyone better."

"Thanks, Matt," Aiden replied. "I hope I've been gauging her feelings right, and she'll say yes."

"According to Emma," Matt said with a smile, "Bailey is crazy about you. I don't think you have anything to worry about."

"So, what about you and Emma?" Aiden asked with a grin. "Do you have any big plans for the future?"

Matt chuckled, then said with youthful confidence, "I'm going to marry her."

Aiden laughed out loud and asked, "Does she know that?"

"Not yet," Matt grinned. "But she will as soon as I ask her!"

* * *

After a few days of scheming, plotting, and working around busy schedules, Aiden and Matt parked a block down the street from the jewelry store and casually walked up the street. Once they were in front of the jewelry store, they quickly ducked inside. Clearly out of their element, they stood in the middle of the lobby for a few minutes, scanning the room. Several minutes later, the salesman walked over and introduced himself.

"Are you gentlemen looking for anything in particular?" the

clerk asked.

Matt appeared to be momentarily tongue-tied, so Aiden replied, "We're both looking for engagement rings for our girlfriends."

"Come this way and I can show you some very nice rings," the clerk suggested.

The two young men spent nearly an hour in the store looking at various rings, debating designs, styles, and colors. They asked each other questions to see if the sisters had ever revealed any particular likes or dislikes when it came to jewelry. Finally concluding that neither girl was into flashy jewelry, both preferring simpler styles, they asked the clerk to show them several different rings to choose from.

Before long, the two men walked out of the store with their purchases safely tucked out of sight in their jacket pockets. They hurried back down the street, got into the pickup, then let out huge sighs of relief.

At the sound of releasing pent-up nerves, the two looked at each other and laughed.

"Well," Matt said as he sank back into the seat of his pickup, "we did it!"

"Yes, we did," Aiden said with a smile. "Do you still like the idea we discussed the other night? Should we ask them both on the same day?"

"I'm game if you are," Matt replied. "This weekend?"

"Let's do it!" Aiden said, as the two young men shook hands, confident of their decisions and their future.

* * *

It was not unusual for family and friends to gather at Travis and Meghan's house in the evenings to hang out and visit. The

Harmon home had been the hub of family activities for years. In the middle of the week, Matt, Todd, and Aiden were sitting around the dining room table having dessert while visiting Travis and Meghan.

"You know," Matt began innocently, "it's been a long time since we've had a big spaghetti dinner. Why don't we have one this weekend? You know, have the whole family over. Invite Mike. It'd be fun."

Meghan smiled at Matt. "I think that's a great idea, Matt! And you're right. We haven't had one in a while. It's about time."

"Aiden and I could help, if you want," Matt offered.

"Honestly, boys," Meghan replied with a chuckle, "the best way you can help would be to stay out of the kitchen. Kaci and I have those dinners down to a science. I'm glad you suggested it, Matt. Make sure you invite your dad and mom too."

"Thanks," Matt said. "I know they would love to be included."

"They're family, Matt," Travis said. "There's no reason not to include them."

"Be sure to invite Bailey and Emma too," Todd suggested. "The more the merrier."

Aiden and Matt looked at each other, then Aiden replied, "We'll ask them. They should be able to come."

Once again, the boys shared a knowing look. The stage had been set.

* * *

It was a beautiful fall day, and the weather was perfect. Leaves were still changing colors but had not yet begun to fall to the ground. Knowing how much Bailey had come to love the gazebo at the park, Aiden had suggested they take a break from work responsibilities and spend some time at the park. Bailey stopped by Aiden's apartment to pick him up, then they swung into the little coffee shop and got two large mugs of hot chocolate.

Once they arrived at the park, Bailey wrapped her light jacket a little tighter, grabbed her hot chocolate in one hand, and took Aiden's hand in the other. They slowly strolled across the park as Bailey marveled at the different species of trees and the natural beauty of the park. As they got to the gazebo, Bailey released Aiden's hand and walked up the steps and over to the railing.

Seeing Bailey leaning against the railing with both hands cupping her mug of hot chocolate, Aiden knew without a doubt this was her happy place. It warmed his heart to see her so happy and at peace.

He sat his hot chocolate down on the picnic table, then walked over to Bailey, putting his arm around her waist. She turned and smiled at him, then returned her gaze to the beauty of the park.

"Are you warm enough, Bailey?" Aiden asked.

"I'm fine," she replied, smiling at him.

The two spent the next half hour simply relaxing against the gazebo railing and enjoying each other's company. They engaged in minimal small talk, content in just being together.

"You remember we're going over to Uncle Travis and Aunt Meghan's house for a spaghetti dinner tonight, right?" Aiden asked.

"I'm really looking forward to it," Bailey replied. "Their spaghetti feeds are so much fun. And it's always nice to be able to hang out with their family. I don't think I've ever met a nicer bunch of people. You're lucky to be part of that family, Aiden."

"I know," he replied, nodding. "They really are the best."

Aiden stepped away from the gazebo railing, and Bailey continued gazing out over the park.

Watching some ducks walk across the park to one of the ponds, Bailey said, "I never get tired of this place. It's so peaceful. And kind of romantic, too."

When Aiden didn't reply, Bailey turned toward the center of the gazebo. There, down on one knee, was Aiden holding out a small box and wearing a wide grin.

Bailey gasped and covered her face with her hands.

"Would you like to join my family?" Aiden asked. "I love you, Bailey. I think I've loved you for a long time. It took getting out of the Army and being away from you before I realized it. I'm so glad God brought you back into my life. Will you marry me?"

"Oh my," she whispered, walking toward him.

Aiden stood and closed the gap between them. Holding out the small ring box, he asked, "What do you say, Bailey? Will you be the answer to all my dreams and be my wife?" Then he added with a chuckle, "My family comes along as part of the deal. We're a package."

Bailey laughed and wrapped her arms around his neck, then gave him a tender kiss as tears streamed down her face. Releasing their embrace, she covered her mouth with her shaking hands as she looked down at the ring.

Looking up into Aiden's expectant face, Bailey said, "Yes. Yes, Aiden, I would love to be your wife. I love you, too. I'm so glad that job offer brought me to Hope."

"I'm glad," Aiden said, laughing. "Otherwise, I probably wouldn't be very good company at dinner tonight."

She chuckled as she said, "I think we'll both be exciting company tonight."

Aiden then removed the ring from the box and slipped it onto her outstretched finger before wrapping her in another tight embrace.

* * *

A few blocks away from the park, Emma pulled her little Honda into a parking space near the batting cages. She jumped out before Matt had a chance to walk around the car to open her door. She grabbed her bat from the back seat and started toward the cages.

"Come on, Matt!" she said. "There's only one empty batting cage. I'm going to go grab it."

Matt laughed as he grabbed his bat and jogged after Emma.

As Matt walked up to the batting cage, Emma looked around the busy park and said, "I wonder why it's so busy here today. We don't normally have any trouble finding an empty cage."

"It's probably because the batting cages and go-karts will be shut down for the season tomorrow," Matt replied.

"Oh!" Emma said in surprise. "I didn't realize that. It's a good thing we decided to come get in a little more practice today, then."

Matt chuckled to himself and said, "The timing was perfect."

Emma didn't waste any time getting the pitching machine set up and began swinging away at baseballs. Matt stood back and watched as she made contact with nearly every pitch. After a few minutes, Emma stepped back to allow Matt a turn.

Before he started the pitching machine, he casually turned to Emma and said, "You remember we're going to Travis and Meghan's tonight for spaghetti, right?"

"How could I forget that?" Emma replied. "I love their spaghetti feeds!"

Matt started the machine and swung at every pitch with a big smile on his face. They traded off every few minutes, alternating between baseballs and softballs.

After nearly an hour of swinging at pitches, Matt shut down the machine and said, "I don't know about you, but I think I'm done."

"Agreed," Emma replied with a smile. "That was a great session."

Emma turned toward the machine to gather up their bats. When she turned back around, Matt was down on one knee, up against the backdrop of the batting cage, holding a small ring box.

Walking toward him, Emma dropped the baseball bats onto the concrete and smiled.

"Emma," Matt said, "I hope you know how much you mean to me. You make me feel complete. I love you, Emma. Will you marry me?"

As a smile quickly took over her entire face, Emma replied, "Well, shortstop, you certainly hit that one out of the park. Yes, I'll marry you!"

Matt jumped up and pulled Emma into his arms. They simply looked into each other's eyes for a moment before Matt leaned down and placed a soft kiss on her lips.

He suddenly pulled away and said, "Wait a minute! I forgot to give you the ring!"

Emma chuckled as she held out her hand, wiggling her empty ring finger. Matt slipped the ring onto her finger, then she grabbed the front of his shirt and pulled him down to eye level.

"Since you forgot the most important part," Emma said grinning, "now you have to kiss me again."

"Yes, ma'am," he replied. "I most certainly do."

Taking Matt by the hand, as they started toward the parking lot, Emma leaned into his shoulder and said, "I love you, too, Matt. I was wondering how long it would take you to figure it out."

Matt chuckled and replied, "I take my time when it's something that's going to last a lifetime."

They were nearly to the car when Emma stopped in her tracks

and slapped her forehead. Running back to the batting cage, she yelled over her shoulder, "We forgot our bats!"

Matt laughed out loud as he waited for his future wife to return. He was just pulling his cell phone out of his pocket when she walked up with a bat slung over each shoulder.

"I'm going to text Aiden and see if he and Bailey want to meet us over at the deli for a sandwich. We can go out to Meghan's whenever we want, but it'll still be several hours before dinner."

Matt got an immediate reply from Aiden, and they all agreed to meet at the deli.

Ten minutes later, Emma pulled her car into the lot and parked a few spaces away from her sister's SUV. Both girls jumped out of their cars and ran to each other with their left hands outstretched.

"Look!" the girls screamed simultaneously. They stopped and looked at the new rings on each other's fingers, then began hugging and talking excitedly at the same time.

Aiden and Matt simply stood back and took it all in.

"I don't know, Matt," Aiden said with mock concern, "do they seem happy to you?"

"Well, Aiden," Matt chuckled, "does loud mean happy? If so, then they must be ecstatic!"

The guys walked over to the girls just as their initial excitement was winding down.

Bailey reached out and slapped Aiden on the arm. "Why didn't you tell me Matt was going to propose to Emma?"

Not one to be left out, Emma slapped Matt's arm. "And why didn't you tell me Aiden was proposing to Bailey?"

"We wanted it to be a surprise," Matt said as he shrugged his shoulders.

"Uh, surprise?" Aiden added with a smile.

Emma squeezed Matt's arm, then jumped back suddenly and said, "Hey, since we got engaged on the same day, why don't we have a double wedding ceremony?"

Aiden and Matt looked at each other and shrugged. "Sure, why not?" Matt replied.

"Whatever you ladies want," Aiden agreed. "We just want you to be happy."

Bailey nodded as she hugged her younger sister. "Then a double wedding ceremony it is!"

"Oh!" Emma exclaimed. "We have to call Dad and Mom! They are going to be so surprised!"

"Right!" Bailey agreed. "Then we'll have to go shopping for wedding dresses! Can't you just hear Dad now? 'What? Two weddings? Here, just take my wallet and bring me whatever is left.' I just wish I could see his face!"

Laughing, Emma walked over and kissed Matt on the cheek. "Matt, will you go inside and order me a sandwich and iced tea so we can call Dad and Mom?"

"Sure," Matt replied with a smile. "Come on, Aiden, let's go get these ladies something to eat. They could be on the phone for a while."

Chapter Nineteen

The Harmon house was filled with family and friends, punctuated by the aroma of simmering spaghetti sauce and baking garlic bread. Meghan looked around the living and family rooms and smiled. This was what she always dreamed family would be. She was happiest when she was surrounded by family. That was one reason everyone knew Travis and Meghan had an open-door policy at their home. Friends, family, and people who simply needed someone, were always welcome.

Even though it was football season, Todd, Travis, and JC were talking baseball with Mike. Jason was playing a video game with his kids while Kaci was helping Meghan and Nicole in the kitchen. Amy was bouncing a happy Levi on her lap in the rocking chair, where he had a good view of his large family. Not wanting to attract undue attention to the girls' fingers, Aiden, Matt, Bailey, and Emma were huddled around the game table in the family room playing a game of Trivial Pursuit.

It was amazing anyone heard the knock at the door over the uproar in the house. But Travis heard it and looked around the room to see who might be missing.

"That must be John and Vicki," Travis said to no one in particular as he walked toward the door. Travis opened the door and welcomed Matt and Amy's parents.

"Come on in and join the noise," he said laughing. "I'm glad you guys were able to come."

"Thanks for inviting us, Travis," John said as he shook Travis's hand.

Vicki held up two tubs of ice cream as she started toward the kitchen. "We brought ice cream for dessert, so I'd better get it in the freezer. Then I have to see my grandson!"

Matt leaned over to Aiden and said quietly, "Now that Dad and Mom are here, do you think we should do this before the craziness of dinner gets started?"

"Sure," Aiden replied. "That's a good idea. Do you want to get people's attention? I'll give Ryleigh a quick call and get her on the phone."

Matt grinned and said, "I can do that."

Walking toward the middle of the living room, Matt smiled and said, "Can I ask a question?"

Todd laughed from across the room and replied, "I don't think dinner is ready yet, Matt!"

As expected, Matt had gotten everyone's attention.

"Actually," Matt said with a grin, "that's not what's on my mind."

Travis laughed and asked, "Are you sure you're feeling okay, Matt? Food is always on your mind."

"Trust me," Matt said, laughing, "when dinner is ready, I'll eat my fair share!"

Matt nodded toward Aiden, who joined him in the middle of the room.

"Aiden and I wanted to tell you all something," Matt began. "That's why we suggested a family spaghetti feed. It would get everyone together in the same place."

"So, I've been conned!" Meghan said with a laugh.

"And I have Ryleigh on the phone," Aiden said as he held up his phone.

"Hi, everybody!" Ryleigh said from the phone. "I'm as confused as usual, so I'll just hang on the phone until I figure out what's going on."

"As you all know," Matt began, "there have been a lot of changes happening for me and Aiden in the past few months. We've been building dreams as fast as we've been building houses. And it's been fantastic! Earlier today we both started building a new dream – one we hope will last the rest of our lives."

Aiden nodded at the girls and motioned them over to stand beside them.

Smiles broke out around the room as people began to suspect what was coming.

Matt reached for Emma's hand just as Aiden reached out and took Bailey's hand while switching his cell phone to the other hand.

"Today I asked Emma to marry me," Matt said with a smile. "And she said yes!"

Aiden raised his and Bailey's clasped hands in the air and added, "And today I asked Bailey to marry me!"

From the corner of the room, JC said with a chuckle, "Don't tell me she actually agreed to marry you, cuz."

Bailey laughed as she gave Aiden a hug. "Yes, JC, I did agree to marry him!"

A loud squeal erupted from Aiden's cell phone. He laughed and said, "Well, it sounds like Ryleigh approves!"

"Yes! Yes! Yes!" Ryleigh yelled from the phone. "I wish I was there so I could hug each one of you. For the record, no more major family announcements are allowed until I'm home and can celebrate with you all in person!"

Meghan looked around the room and said, "This family is

growing every day, Ryleigh, so you'd better hurry and get home!"

"Soon. Very soon," she replied. "But now I need to go. Congratulations, Aiden and Bailey, and Matt and Emma! You guys are going to be so happy together!"

Within minutes, the four young adults were being mobbed as everyone crowded in to congratulate them and ask questions.

John and Vicki walked up to Matt and Emma and gave them both a hug. "Congratulations, son," John said. "We're very happy for you both. And this is one wedding we're not going to miss!"

After about fifteen minutes, Aaron and Sophie realized their dad had abandoned the video game they were playing. They walked over to where everyone was gathered in the middle of the living room and looked around.

"What's all the excitement?" Aaron asked.

Kaci looked at her nine-year-old twins and smiled. "Didn't you hear? Aiden and Bailey and Matt and Emma are going to get married."

"Oh," Aaron replied, unimpressed.

"We already knew that," Sophie added.

Everyone looked at them in confusion, including the newly engaged couples.

"What do you mean you already knew that?" Kaci asked her kids. "They just told us."

"It's easy," Aaron said, shrugging his shoulders. "Uncle Matt always goes to the batting cages with Emma. He doesn't take any other girls batting."

"And Aiden always goes to the park with Bailey," Sophie added, wondering why this was so difficult for the grownups to understand.

"Besides," Aaron added, "they look at each other with googly eyes all the time. That usually means someone's getting married."

The room erupted with laughter as Mike chimed in, "It makes

perfect sense. We adults tend to overcomplicate things."

Aaron and Sophie started walking back to their video game, then stopped halfway across the room.

"I assume we get to be in the wedding," Aaron stated logically. "Sophie is a really good flower girl and I'm the best ring bearer around. Besides, Levi is too little to be the ring bearer."

A second round of laughter erupted before Kaci said, "Why don't we just let them choose their own flower girls and ring bearers?"

"Okay," Aaron said with the logic only a nine-year-old could muster with a straight face. "But I'm telling you, we already know what we're doing."

Emma walked over to Aaron and put her hand on his shoulder, seeming to be deep in thought. "I don't know, Bales," she said, looking at her sister. "They *are* experienced, they live right here in town, and they're both pretty cute."

"I'm handsome," Aaron corrected. "Sophie's cute."

"Oh, right," Emma said, properly chastised. "Handsome and cute. Got it. We don't have any nieces or nephews. What do you say, Bales?"

Bailey walked over and looked the two kids up and down. Then she spun Sophie around, much to the little girl's delight, and said, "Yes, Emma, I think these two will do just fine."

Aaron nodded in satisfaction and said, "Told you." Then he walked back and picked up his video game.

The twins were the undoing of every adult in the room. Once they began to regain their composure, Travis said, "Since all this just happened today, I assume you haven't had time to discuss any details yet."

Emma put her arm around Matt's waist and replied, "We decided one thing. We're going to have a double wedding ceremony!"

"Uh, make that two things," Bailey corrected, looking across the room at Aaron and Sophie. "We know who the flower girl and ring bearer will be!"

"As you can imagine," Aiden said, "we will have a lot of details to work out and questions to answer."

"Right," Matt agreed. "But the first question is: when's dinner?"

Meghan walked over and gave Matt a big hug. "Give us twenty minutes to finish the spaghetti, then you can eat, Matt. I promise!"

Mike walked toward the kitchen laughing and shaking his head. "I don't think that boy ever gets full! He shouldn't be building houses. He should be running a restaurant!"

"And eat up all the profits?" Todd said. "I don't think so!"

* * *

After enjoying a relaxing weekend with family, Aiden and Matt jumped back on the house project, knowing they would be running out of good weather before long. The self-imposed goal they had for completing the outside of Roger's house was Thanksgiving. While waiting for the delayed delivery of siding, besides completing some small commercial projects, they managed to install all the windows and exterior doors at the house.

Now that the siding had been delivered, they had a full crew working to get it installed. Part of the crew was putting up the siding, while others followed behind doing the caulking and other prep work to get ready for painting. The end of the week was supposed to bring a couple of warmer days that would provide the last opportunity to get the exterior of the house painted before colder weather set in.

Aiden and Matt were moving some scaffolding into place at

the side of the house when a pickup with an R & M Development logo on the side pulled up along the curb. Two men climbed out of the truck and started walking toward the house.

"Hey, Mike!" Matt and Aiden said simultaneously.

Shaking hands with the second man, Aiden said, "It's good to see you again, Roger."

Roger patted Matt on the back as he surveyed the house in front of him. "I've got to give you guys credit. I'm amazed at the progress you've made."

Roger walked toward the house, followed by Mike, Matt, and Aiden, and began assessing the work that had been done. As he walked around the house, nodding his head in satisfaction, he was careful to avoid the men who were hard at work.

On the back side of the house, Roger stood back as he watched the crew work. When he saw how quickly the prep crew went to work when a section of siding had been installed, he nodded his head, then walked over to the young contractors.

"I'm impressed," Roger said. "I'm very impressed. You guys appear to have a great crew. Now I see why the house is as far along as it is. Honestly, I didn't expect much to be done before spring."

"Our goal is to finish the exterior of the house before the cold weather sets in," Matt said. "That way we'll be able to work on the interior during the winter."

"We've been hustling, hoping to catch those last few warm days later this week to be able to paint," Aiden added.

Roger turned to Mike and said, "You were right, Mike. These guys are naturals."

"I don't know that I'd call us naturals," Matt said modestly. "Maybe we're quick learners. We've learned so much from Todd, Meghan, and Travis. They not only taught us how to do the work, but they also taught us how to manage crews and work with subcontractors."

"Matt's right," Aiden added. "We wouldn't even be able to do this if it weren't for them mentoring us."

"I like it when people are humble enough to give credit where credit is due," Roger said. "Well, there's no doubt, you two are good students."

"Well, boys," Mike said as he shook Aiden's hand and patted Matt on the back, "we better get out of here and let you get back to work. It looks good, really good. We need to meet up at Luigi's for lunch one of these days when you have time."

"That sounds great, Mike!" Matt replied. "Even if we're busy, we still have to eat."

"I figured you might see it that way," Mike replied with a laugh.

Roger shook hands with the young men and said, "Thanks for letting us steal a few minutes of your time."

"Anytime, Roger," Aiden replied with a smile.

Roger and Mike walked back to the pickup, climbed in, and began talking as they looked over at the development.

"So, what do you think?" Mike asked his friend.

"Their first house was quite impressive," Roger replied. "I was surprised at how much they've already done on this house. As I told them, I honestly didn't expect a lot of progress before spring. They're hard workers, there's no doubt about that. I'm anxious to see the completed exterior later this week. I figure one or both of us could stop by occasionally throughout the winter and check on their progress. If this house lives up to my expectations after seeing their first house and how they work, I think we may have found our general contractors for the development. And the fact that they're young men just starting out is a bonus. I like giving start-ups a chance to prove themselves."

"I don't think we'll be disappointed," Mike said. "And I

know they rely heavily on Todd, Meghan, and Travis's experience and expertise. They aren't afraid to ask questions when they aren't sure about something."

"Didn't you tell me you've known Matt since he was in high school?" Roger asked.

"That's right," Mike answered. "He was one of the kids who frequented JC's Hope right after it opened. He willingly admits the youth center probably saved him from heading down a destructive path. He's a good kid, but he had a rough time of it growing up. Both his parents were alcoholics, but he's turned into quite a young man. In fact, he's partly responsible for helping his parents get clean. He and Aiden hired Matt's dad as a laborer, and I can honestly say John is a changed man."

Roger nodded in understanding. "And Aiden is Todd's son, right?"

"Right," Mike replied. "He served in the Army Corps of Engineers, then helped with some of the construction at the youth center when he got out of the service."

"Perfect," Roger said, smiling. "Two very impressive young men. I think this is going to work out just fine."

Chapter Twenty

With everyone's busy lives, the holidays were upon them before they knew it. JC and Amy wanted to have the big family Christmas at their new home, especially since it would be Levi's first Christmas. So, it was decided Travis and Meghan would host Thanksgiving, and JC and Amy would host Christmas. Bailey and Emma's family hadn't had an opportunity to see them since they'd gotten engaged, so they were invited to spend the Thanksgiving holiday in Hope. Although Meghan insisted there was plenty of room at their house for the Campbell clan, the girls' parents said they would stay at the Hope Inn. They'd already made reservations for themselves and the boys.

Ryleigh made it home the day before Thanksgiving, so she and other family members had gathered at the five-acre parcel to decide who would get which piece of the property. Travis, Meghan, Todd, and Nicole joined the younger adults on the parcel beside JC and Amy's house.

"Okay, kids," Todd said as he pointed toward some stakes at various locations on the property. "As you can see, all four parcels have been surveyed and staked out. Obviously, JC and Amy's parcel is already claimed. The remaining three parcels belong to Ryleigh, Aiden and Bailey, and Matt and Emma. You can walk around and see what you think. All the parcels are the same size, an acre and a quarter, so size shouldn't be a concern. There will also be an easement taken out down the middle of the property to allow for a road to access the two back parcels. So, it's just a matter of whether someone prefers a particular location on the property. So, wander around, discuss it among yourselves and with each other, then let us know what you decide. We'll be hanging out over here."

For the next half hour, the young adults wandered around the property, mostly staying together as one group to discuss things. They eventually met up in the middle of the property, pointing in different directions, then finally shaking hands with each other. They were all wearing smiles as they walked back to where the older adults were sitting on the tailgates of their pickups.

"Well," Meghan began, "what did you kids decide? You're all smiling, so we assume everyone is happy with your decisions."

"The only one who really had a preference for the location was Matt," Aiden said. "He wanted to be beside JC and Amy, and the rest of us are perfectly fine with that."

"Thanks, everyone," Matt said as he put his arm around Emma's waist. "I really appreciate that."

"Ryleigh didn't have a preference at all," Aiden said. "So, she and I actually flipped a coin to decide. Bailey and I will take the parcel directly behind JC and Amy, and Ryleigh will take the one behind Matt and Emma."

"Okay," Todd said, nodding. "That sounds great. We'll get the paperwork drawn up to have ownership of those parcels transferred to you kids. Thanks for making it easy."

"I just want to thank you again for this," Matt said seriously. "You guys have been amazing. I can't believe how you've taken me into your family as if I were just another one of your kids. Thank you."

"Now we'll have to get Roger's house finished so we can get started on our homes!" Aiden said with a chuckle.

"There's not much chance we'll get them built before we get married," Matt said. "But it's sure nice to already have the land."

"Have you kids given any thought to when you plan to have the wedding?" Meghan asked.

Bailey and Emma looked at each other, then looked over at the guys. "We haven't decided on an actual date yet," Bailey said, "but we're thinking sometime next summer."

"That gives you a few months to work out all the details," Travis said. "Just be sure to let us know if you need any help from us for anything."

Matt grinned and said, "Well, we sure wouldn't turn down any help working on Roger's house."

"That's a given, Matt," Todd replied. "Travis and I have already cut back to part-time, so we'll have plenty of time to help you boys out. Not only on Roger's house, but also on your own homes and any other house-building projects that come along."

"If we're done here," Meghan said, "why don't we go back over to the house?" Looking at Bailey and Emma, she continued, "Your family should be arriving pretty soon, right?"

"Yeah," Emma answered. "In fact, they may already be in town. I'll text the boys and find out."

"Tell them to come out to the house whenever they want," Meghan suggested. "We're planning to go over to Luigi's for pizza tonight, and we'd love to have your family join us."

Emma began texting back and forth with Spencer, and her suspicions were correct. The family had arrived in Hope less than twenty minutes earlier. Bailey and Emma were going to meet up with them at the Hope Inn, then the entire Campbell family would come back to the Harmon home for the afternoon, followed by dinner at Luigi's.

* * *

When Bailey pulled her SUV into the Harmon driveway on Thanksgiving Day, there were already several vehicles parked there. Her parents pulled in and parked directly behind her.

Joseph and Hannah Campbell stepped out of their car and walked up to join their four adult children. Like her younger daughter, Hannah was shorter than the rest of the family, standing just under five-foot-seven, and had shoulder-length blonde hair. After having rested up from the previous day's drive over the pass, she looked comfortable in a pair of skinny jeans, tall boots, and an oversized sweater. Her husband stood just over six-two and had black hair that was graying at the temples. Now in his mid-50s, his mustache and goatee were more gray than black.

Looking around, Hannah said, "They must have a large family. There are already more cars here than we've ever had at our townhouse in Seattle."

Emma walked up beside her mom and said, "You're right, they do have a large family. At least you met a few of them last night, so they won't all be new faces to remember today."

Wyatt and Spencer didn't wait for the rest of their family. They started up the driveway, stepped onto the porch, and walked in the front door like they had been doing it their entire lives.

Hannah shook her head and said, "You'd think we raised those boys without any manners at all. They didn't even knock!"

Joseph Campbell took his wife's hand and started up the driveway. "Don't worry so much, dear. Travis and Meghan told us last night to just come on in when we got here. That's exactly what the boys did."

Hannah laughed. "I guess I've been in the city too long. I've lost some of the open hospitality of my country upbringing."

189

Even though she was a bit hesitant, Hannah followed her daughters into the house without knocking. Her husband put his hand on her back and smiled as they joined the others in the festive home.

Meghan and Travis immediately went to welcome their guests. Travis shook hands with Joseph, and Meghan wrapped Hannah in a friendly hug.

"Welcome to our home once again," Meghan said, smiling. "We're so glad you were able to come over for the holiday. And I'm glad we didn't scare you off yesterday. We have quite a boisterous bunch at times. I think everyone is here, so let me introduce you to the rest of the family." She then whispered, "I promise, there won't be a quiz at the end of the day."

Travis raised his hand in the middle of the living room. "Hey, everybody, we want to introduce you to Bailey and Emma's family. Make them feel welcome."

"Okay, everybody," Meghan began with a laugh. "Stay put. Don't be moving around so I end up introducing the same person three times."

"Would we do that, Mom?" Josh asked innocently.

"Yes, you would!" Meghan replied with a chuckle "So everyone stay right where you are."

Turning to the Campbells, Meghan said, "This is Joseph and Hannah Campbell, the girls' parents. And there's Wyatt and Spencer, their brothers. You can figure out who is who on your own! And, of course, you all know Bailey and Emma."

Looking around the room at her family, Meghan turned to Hannah and apologized. "I hope this doesn't seem too overwhelming to you. I'll try to make it as easy as possible."

Hannah smiled and said, "Not a problem, Meghan. I'm pretty good with names."

"Okay," Meghan began with a smile. "When I say your name,

raise your hand. Last night you met Todd, Nicole, Ryleigh, and of course Aiden and Matt. So that leaves our daughter Kaci, her husband Jason, and their twins Aaron and Sophie. Over there is our son Josh, his wife Amy, and their little boy Levi. John and Vicki Phoenix are Amy and Matt's parents. And last, but certainly not least, the guy trying to hide behind Matt, and failing miserably, is Mike Slater. Mike is a very dear friend, and we consider him family. Did I forget anyone?"

"Good job, honey," Travis said. "I think you got everyone. It sure helped that they met a few last night."

Joseph raised his hand in greeting and said, "It's nice to meet all of you. Thank you so much for inviting us for the holiday. We're looking forward to getting to know you. And I hope you'll show us the houses the boys are working on. The girls have told us a lot about them. Oh, by the way, I could smell that Thanksgiving dinner as soon as I pulled into the driveway! I'm looking forward to that too!"

"Since you guys are staying for the weekend," Bailey said to her parents, "we thought we would let you relax today, then show you the houses tomorrow."

"That sounds good to me," Joseph replied. "Based on the smells coming from the kitchen, I doubt I'll be able to move much after dinner anyway!"

* * *

After spending a relaxing Thanksgiving Day at Travis and Meghan's, everyone agreed to meet next door at JC and Amy's house Friday afternoon. The Campbells would be able to see the first house Matt and Aiden built before going over to the house under construction.

Most of the family visited on the back deck while JC and

Amy gave the Campbells the grand tour of their home. Hannah fell in love with the kitchen, and Joseph commented several times about the spaciousness of the home compared to their townhouse in Seattle. Wyatt and Spencer abandoned the home tour partway through in favor of visiting with the others on the deck.

As they met on the deck at the back of the house, Joseph said, "You boys have done a fine job on this house. I'm very impressed! And to think this was the first house you built. That's incredible!"

"We had a lot of help from Dad and Travis," Aiden said. "A lot of other people helped out too. In fact, I don't know if they told you or not, but even Bailey and Emma helped us install some of the siding and helped with the final touchup work."

"They did mention that," Joseph confirmed. "It really didn't surprise me. Those two never quite adapted to city life. Any time they can do something outside in the fresh air, especially if it involves learning something new, they usually jump in with both feet."

"I just love Amy's kitchen!" Hannah said. "You boys must've had a woman's influence in the design of that kitchen. It's perfect!"

"Meghan helped with that," Matt said with a smile. "You probably don't know this, but she designed their house next door, and has done design work on the side for years."

"Really?" Hannah said in surprise, looking at Meghan. "That's amazing. You can certainly tell both these homes have had a woman's touch."

Meghan laughed. "It comes with growing up in the family construction business. You learn a lot of things that most people don't learn as kids."

"She's overly modest, Hannah," Travis said with a chuckle. "She not only does design work, but she's also a very skilled carpenter and an expert heavy equipment operator. In fact, I met her when she was operating a bulldozer on our property next door. That was her property, and she was getting ready to build the house when we met."

Hannah and Joseph shook their heads in amazement. "You have quite a family here," Joseph said.

"God has been good to us," Travis replied as he hugged his wife. "Well, should we head over to the other house? Mike said he would meet us there. Then we can all come back to our house and enjoy Thanksgiving leftovers for dinner. How does that sound?"

"I think I'll ride with Matt and Emma," Spencer said quickly. "If I stick with Matt, I know I'll make it back to the food!"

Emma laughed at her brother as she took him by the arm. "It didn't take you long to figure Matt out. Stick with us, Spence, and I guarantee you'll get fed."

Mike was waiting at the second house when the caravan of vehicles pulled up along the curb about twenty minutes later. People piled out of cars and pickups and began scattering in different directions around the house. Mike shook hands with Joseph and Hannah and chuckled at the others.

"And…they're off!" Mike said to Joseph as he laughed.

Everyone was talking excitedly as they explained different aspects of the construction project to the Campbells. Once they had seen the entire outside of the house, Mike asked if they wanted to see the inside, which he warned was basically the framework.

"I want to see inside!" Wyatt said. "I looked through the windows, but it would be cool to go inside and look around."

"Well, I've got the key," Mike said. "Let's take a tour."

As the group approached the front door, Aiden cautioned everyone, "Now be careful. These are just temporary steps at both the front and back doors, but it makes it easier to get in and out of the house while we're working."

People filed in the front door one at a time and began exploring the interior of the house.

"Look, I'm Casper the Friendly Ghost!" Spencer said as he walked through one of the walls.

"How old are you, Spence?" Bailey asked, shaking her head. "Aaron and Sophie are acting more mature than you are!"

Spencer simply smiled as he walked through another wall. "Well, they've grown up around construction, so this is probably boring to them. Walking through walls is a new experience for me."

Aaron walked over to Spencer and whispered, "It's okay, Spence. I still have fun walking through the walls, and it's not boring at all."

Before long, everyone had done all the exploring they wanted to do, so they began heading back to the vehicles. Mike was standing on the sidewalk in front of the house talking to Joseph and some of the other men. Joseph was curious about the development and wondered how many homes it would have.

"There will be about a dozen homes once the development is complete," Mike said. "That's the first phase. There may be a second phase that will include a few more homes, but Roger hasn't made a definite decision on that yet. Time will tell."

Travis and Todd looked at each other with a smile, then shrugged their shoulders. Before long, the entire gang had loaded into various vehicles and headed toward the Harmon home to enjoy leftover turkey sandwiches.

Chapter Twenty-One

Not long after Thanksgiving, the entire Byers and Harmon clan made their annual trek to the mountains to cut down Christmas trees. They made a day of it, taking along sleds and inner tubes so they could go sledding as well. When Bailey and Emma's brothers heard about the plans, they asked if they could join them. After being assured they were always welcome, Wyatt and Spencer drove over from Seattle the afternoon before, armed with warm clothes and a brand-new sled.

It didn't take long for everyone to find the perfect tree for their home. As he always did, Todd brought along his pickup to haul the trees home. Before long, six trees had been loaded into his truck and tied down for the return trip. Then sleds and inner tubes were unloaded from Travis's pickup, and everyone began dragging them up the hill for an afternoon of sledding.

Wyatt and Spencer whooped and hollered on every run down the hill, much to the delight of Aaron and Sophie. On several runs, Aaron had convinced Spencer to let him ride along on his sled. So, Aaron perched himself in front of Spencer on the sled and they sped down the hill, yelling at the top of their lungs.

After completing one such run, Spencer had just reached down to give Aaron a high-five when he got smacked in the back with a snowball. Turning around, Spencer spied Wyatt looking very guilty as he tried to hide behind his sisters. Sleds were abandoned along the snowy hill in favor of a massive snowball fight. Everyone got involved in the fray. There was no choosing up sides. It was open warfare.

At one point, Aaron had managed to sneak around behind Wyatt and blasted him with a snowball.

"That's from Spence!" Aaron yelled with a smile as he took off running through the snow.

Wyatt laughed and said, "Don't worry, Spence, I'll get even with you. I know where you sleep!"

By the end of the afternoon, after countless trips down the hill, an hour-long snowball fight, and a lot of wrestling and playing in the snow, everyone was exhausted. They retrieved all the inner tubes and sleds from where they had been abandoned along the hill and got them loaded into the back of Travis's truck.

Jason, Aiden, and JC had a fire going in the fire pit and they were setting things up to roast hotdogs and marshmallows. Meghan had brought along several large thermoses filled with hot chocolate. The next hour or so was spent with everyone huddled around the fire pit roasting hotdogs, toasting marshmallows, and drinking hot chocolate as they warmed up. As the sun began to dip lower in the sky, they gathered their belongings, extinguished the fire, and headed down the mountain, another fun holiday tradition in the books.

* * *

All the family homes were decked out in full Christmas attire. Wreaths hung on the doors, colorful lights hung from the eaves of the houses, and various Christmas figures graced the snow-covered lawns. Inside, the homes were equally festive, with

Christmas decorations adorning nearly every room, and a huge Christmas tree being the focal point of the living areas.

JC and Amy went all out decorating their new home since it was Levi's first Christmas. Meghan and Kaci spearheaded a group to help with food preparation, and Bailey and Emma had the full-time job of keeping Aiden and Matt from peeking at the presents under the tree.

Amy and Matt's parents would be joining them for Christmas and had dropped off gifts for everyone on Christmas Eve. The Campbell family had been invited to come over for Christmas but opted out at the last minute because of a snowstorm on the pass.

Matt was pacing back and forth in front of the living room window, watching for Kaci's family. He was sure they would begin opening gifts as soon as Aaron and Sophie arrived.

"There's Jason, Kaci, and the kids!" Matt said excitedly. "Now we can open presents, right?"

Meghan laughed as she replied, "No, Matt. We still need to wait for your parents and Mike. Don't worry, we won't let the elves make off with your gifts!"

Mike pulled into JC and Amy's driveway, followed by John and Vicki. Matt rushed to the door in an effort to hurry people along.

"What's the hurry, son?" John asked with a laugh.

"We can't open any presents until everyone's here," Matt said with a grin. Turning to Meghan, he said, "They're here now. We can start, right?"

"Calm down, Matt," JC laughed. "You've had Christmas here before. You know the rules. One person at a time."

Mike walked over and put his arm around Matt's shoulder. "What do you say, Meghan? He looks a bit sad. We can't have sad kids at Christmastime. Maybe after the little kids open their gifts, you know, Levi, Aaron, and Sophie, then Matt can be the first of the big kids to open gifts?"

Several of the adults quickly met in the middle of the room for a group discussion. They were whispering and waving their arms theatrically while they looked over at Matt, seeming to have a hard time making a decision. The other adults looked on smiling.

The meeting broke up and Meghan walked toward the Christmas tree.

"Okay," Meghan began seriously, "after much deliberation, the committee decided Matt could open gifts right after the younger kids."

Matt pumped his fist in the air in victory and yelled, "Yes!"

Emma slapped her forehead with her hand and shook her head, laughing.

"Just remember, Emma," Aiden said without sympathy, "you're the one who agreed to marry him."

"I know, I know," Emma said, laughing. "Life sure won't be boring!"

Following another long-standing family tradition, once everyone had found a seat and had settled in, Todd and Kaci began passing out the gifts. Being only four months old, Levi didn't open many gifts, but he had lots of help from Sophie and Aaron. He was perfectly content being passed around among his parents, grandparents, uncles, and aunts. It didn't take Aaron and Sophie long to rip open their gifts and begin playing. Within about an hour, all the gifts had been opened and there was a huge pile of wrapping paper in the middle of the room, which JC and John gathered and stuffed into garbage bags.

After the chaos of opening gifts, everyone settled in to enjoy a relaxing Christmas day. Lots of pictures were being taken, and some of the people newer to the family spent time getting to know each other. JC and Emma found their way to the piano in the family room and filled the house with Christmas music. By mid-afternoon, some of the younger crowd went outside to play in the snow and build snowmen before being called in for Christmas dinner.

By the time dinner was over, Levi was fast asleep in his playpen in the corner of the family room, not far from the Christmas tree. Even with all the noise, Vicki marveled at how easily her grandson had fallen asleep.

Travis walked over and joined John and Vicki on the sofa.

"Did you have a good time today?" Travis asked with a chuckle. "Or was this family a bit overwhelming?"

John sank back into the sofa, looked around the room, and sighed. "You know, Travis," he began, "all those years wasted. I had no idea what we were missing out on. You have an amazing family. You're a very lucky man."

"Not lucky, John," Travis replied. "Blessed. So incredibly blessed."

John nodded as a lone tear formed in the corner of his eye. "I'm glad Amy and Matt are part of your family now. They couldn't do any better."

"Remember, John," Travis said as he put his hand on John's arm, "you and Vicki are part of this family now, too."

"Thanks, Travis," John replied quietly. "For everything. And thanks for inviting us to share the holiday with you and your family. God truly is good."

* * *

With the holidays behind them, and no big commercial projects on the books until spring, Matt and Aiden focused their energies on completing the interior of Roger's house. They wanted to have the house finished by spring since they now knew they would be building their own homes soon.

All indications were that it would be a very busy year for the family. Homes to build for Aiden and Matt, several large commercial projects coming up for the construction company, and a double wedding to plan.

When Aiden pulled onto the lot to begin work on Roger's house, there were already two other Byers Construction trucks, as well as Matt's pickup on site. He grabbed his hard hat and toolbelt and started toward the front of the house. Once inside, he stood with his hands on his hips, looked around and simply shook his head. There was a full crew already hard at work. At a quick glance, it looked like Travis and Todd had finished most of the electrical work, and the drywall installation was progressing rapidly.

Aiden walked up behind Matt, who was cutting a piece of drywall, and tapped him on the back.

Matt turned around and smiled. "Glad to see you could make it, buddy."

"All it takes is a couple hours at the shop to make someone feel like a slacker over here," Aiden said with a laugh. "You guys have been making a lot of headway. I had to take care of a few things, then I left Steve in charge of the shop. He'll call me if he needs something."

"Not a problem, Aiden," Matt said. "I was just jerking your chain a bit. Even though it's the slow season at the shop, you've still been wearing two hats since Todd went to part-time. But I swear he's working harder now than he was before he semi-retired. He's spending a ton of time working over here."

"You're right," Aiden agreed. "I don't know how he and Uncle Travis do it. Where is Dad, anyway?"

"He's back in one of the bedrooms helping with drywall," Matt replied.

"Where do you want me to get started?" Aiden asked, looking around.

"Pretty much everyone is working on drywall right now," Matt said. "So, I guess pick a room and see who can use the extra set of hands."

Aiden walked into one of the back bedrooms and found his dad and John just finishing the last piece of Sheetrock on the ceiling.

"It looks like I got here just in time," Aiden said with a chuckle. "Hanging drywall on the ceiling is one of my least favorite things."

"You always did have impeccable timing, son," Todd said laughing. "Are you here to help us with this bedroom?"

"Whatever you need, Dad," Aiden replied. "I'm here to help."

"Everything okay down at the shop?" Todd asked.

"Yep," Aiden replied. "I had a couple fires to put out with mixed-up orders, but everything's good. Steve said he'd call me if he had any questions."

They both turned toward the door just as John returned, carrying a sheet of drywall.

"Where do you want to start on the wall, Todd?" John asked.

Pointing toward the corner of the room, Todd said, "Why don't we start in that corner, John? Now that Aiden's here, we should be able to knock out this room in no time."

* * *

Over the next few weeks, the house inched closer to completion. Travis and Todd both enjoyed working on the house and seeing the growth in Aiden and Matt as they began to take control of their project. Roger and Mike stopped by at least once a week to check on the progress and were pleased with the quality of the work.

By the time the ground was beginning to dry out from the wet winter, the interior of Roger's house was nearly complete. The temporary porches had been removed from the front and back doors as they began to build the permanent structures. Matt and his dad were working on the front porch and small deck area when Roger and Mike pulled up along the curb.

"Hey, Matt," Mike said as the two men approached the front of the house.

Matt and his dad stopped what they were doing and stood to shake hands with Mike and Roger.

"You guys must be just about finished with the house," Roger said as he looked around.

"Pretty close," Matt said with a smile. "We should be done by the end of the week. We wanted to wait until the ground dried out a little before we built the porches. Although it would have been nice to have them earlier."

Roger nodded his head in satisfaction. "Is it okay if we go inside to take a look around?"

"Sure," Matt said. "There's a box of disposable shoe covers right inside the door. That way we can protect the flooring from all the dirt."

As they started into the house, Roger turned and asked, "By the way, is Aiden around?"

"I think he's working on the back porch," John said.

"What about Travis and Todd? Are they here?" Roger asked nonchalantly.

"They both happen to be in the house flagging things for touchup," Matt said. "You should run into them in there somewhere."

About twenty minutes later, Todd poked his head out the front door where Matt was still working on the porch.

"Hey, Matt," Todd said, "will you go around back and get Aiden? Then can you two boys join us in the kitchen for a few minutes?"

Matt looked confused, but said, "Sure. We'll be right in."

Less than five minutes later, Aiden and Matt stepped in the front door, each grabbing a pair of disposable shoe covers, and met the other men in the kitchen.

"Hey, Dad," Aiden said with a confused look on his face. "What's up? Is there a problem?"

Mike chuckled and said, "You could say that."

Matt and Aiden looked back and forth at each other, totally confused. Even looking at Travis and Todd did nothing to ease their confusion.

"You see," Roger said with a smile, "the problem is that you boys do great work."

"I don't understand," Matt said. "If we do great work, how is that a problem?"

Todd jumped in to save the boys from any possible stress. "You see, boys, Roger and Mike have seen the quality of your work, and your work ethic, firsthand. That's a problem. Because now they want to hire you to be the contractors for the entire development!"

"No way!" Matt said in unbelief.

Mike walked over and patted Matt on the back. "Yes way, Matt."

"You're kidding, right?" Aiden asked, still not convinced.

"Not kidding, Aiden," Roger said with a smile. "You boys have quite honestly blown my expectations right out of the water. You have done a phenomenal job on this house. I like your work. I like the way you manage your crews. And I like your integrity. I think you're exactly the type of contractors we want working on our development."

"So, what you do say, boys?" Travis asked, grinning. "Do you want to keep building houses?"

Aiden and Matt looked at each other, then simultaneously yelled, "Oh, yeah!"

Suddenly, Matt's face turned serious. "Wait a minute. We're both getting married this summer."

"Not a problem," Roger said. "Travis and Todd already told us that you'll be getting married, and also building your own homes. I'm sure we can work around your busy schedules."

"And remember, boys," Todd added, "Travis and I are available to help. I'm already finding I don't do retirement, even semi-retirement, very well. I need to stay busy!"

"Well, then," Aiden said, "stick with us, Dad. It sounds like we're about to get very busy!"

A few days later, Matt and Aiden parked their truck in the driveway of Roger's house, and Todd and Travis pulled in beside them. They all got out and went into the house, putting on disposable shoe covers. After spending almost an hour walking through the house and inspecting it for any last-minute touchup that needed to be done, they were satisfied the house was complete.

They walked back out onto the front porch and locked the door behind them.

"I'm glad we're not responsible for the landscaping," Matt said as he looked around at the wet ground.

"I agree," Aiden said, nodding. "I'm glad Roger plans to contract that out to a landscaping company. We'll stick to building houses."

As the four men began walking to their trucks, Matt stopped and looked toward the middle of the development, pointing.

"That's not where that big sign was before," Matt said.

"I think you're right, Matt," Todd said, as the four walked

over to the sign.

"This is a different sign," Travis said with a smile. "Read it."

Matt walked over to face the sign, then began reading. "Coming Soon. Hope Estates – Phase One. R & M Development. Phoenix Rising Homes, General Contractors."

Todd laughed and said, "They didn't waste any time getting a new sign up!"

"Wow," Matt said quietly. Then he pulled Aiden into a big hug. "We did it, Aiden."

"Yes, we did," Aiden replied. Then he added with a laugh, "And apparently we're going to keep doing it!"

Chapter Twenty-Two

It was early in the year, and the ground was still drying out from the wet winter. Aiden and Matt had a few weeks before they would be starting on the second house in the Hope Estates development, and things had not yet picked up at the construction company. Finding they had a bit of time on their hands before life got hectic, it was a good time to concentrate on wedding plans. Since they managed to see Bailey and Emma nearly every day, the four had already discussed some basic plans. Now it was time to get the family involved. So, the girls arranged a weekend when their parents could drive over to meet with the rest of the family for a wedding planning session.

Everyone was settling in at Travis and Meghan's house, anxious to discuss the wedding.

Walking over to Bailey's brothers, Aiden said, "Hey, guys, it's great to see you again. I didn't know you were coming over."

"We came for moral support," Spencer said with a chuckle.

"Moral support?" Aiden asked, confused.

"Yeah," Wyatt laughed. "That, and we thought there might be cake samples."

Matt had walked up and heard Wyatt's comment. "Oh, no

you don't! We have first dibs on any cake. Wait…was there going to be cake?"

Laughing, Aiden said, "The girls have the binder with all the notes. Should we get started?"

"A binder of notes," Spencer laughed. "See, I knew you guys would need us. Wave if you need to be rescued. In the meantime, we'll just hang out over here and be innocent bystanders."

"We'll keep that in mind, Spence," Aiden replied with a chuckle.

Aiden and Matt joined Bailey and Emma on the sofa in the living room.

"Well, kids," Todd began, "why don't you tell us what decisions you've made, and we can go from there?"

After looking at the others on the sofa, Aiden said, "I guess I'll get the ball rolling. A double ceremony seems to have more moving pieces, so we'll try not to make it too confusing. We knew we all wanted a summer wedding, but we just decided on the actual date last night. We'll be getting married on June 24th, so everyone block out your calendars for that day."

"We plan to have the ceremony at Hope Community Church," Bailey said. "That seems like the logical choice since Travis and I both pastor there. I already checked and the church is available." Then she added with a laugh, "Travis since I'm going to be pretty busy that day, we would love it if you could perform the ceremony."

Travis nodded his head and said with a smile, "I would be honored. Thanks for asking."

"We never considered anyone else," Bailey said. "If it weren't for you, Emma and I wouldn't even be here in Hope. So, thank you!"

Aiden reached over and took Bailey's hand in his. "Since it's going to be a double wedding, there will be plenty of people involved, so we decided we're not going to have a lot of bridesmaids and groomsmen. We'll try to keep it simple. We're going to let everyone announce their own attendants, then we'll discuss some of the other details."

Turning to Todd, Aiden said, "Dad, obviously I want you to be my best man. You've been my best man since the day I was born. No sense changing that now."

Todd smiled and said, "Thanks, son. I can't think of anything I'd rather do."

"Meghan," Bailey began, "you took me and Emma into your home when we came to town, even though we were complete strangers to you, and you made us feel like family. I've had so much fun getting to know you and your family. I would love for you to be my matron of honor."

"Of course, Bailey," Meghan said. "I'd love to."

Matt looked over at his dad and said, "Dad, I really want you to be my best man."

John looked up at his son and asked, "Are you sure, Matt? I doubt I deserve that honor."

"Yes, Dad, I'm sure," Matt replied with a smile.

"Amy," Emma said, looking over at her friend, "since I came to work at JC's Hope, you've become one of my best friends. I enjoy working with you, and I've had so much fun getting to know you on a personal level. I would be honored if you would agree to be my matron of honor."

"Wow, Emma," Amy replied quietly. "Thank you so much. I would love to."

Aiden looked across the room at his young cousins and smiled. "As for the flower girl and ring bearer, Aaron made it pretty clear that he and Sophie were the only logical choices, so that was never a question."

Bailey looked at her dad and smiled. "Well, Dad, marrying

off both daughters in one day. I think you're getting a deal there. Two weddings for the price of one! Emma and I would be honored to have you walk us both down the aisle. Two arms, two daughters. That seems to work out just about right."

Joseph wiped a stray tear from his eye and said, "I can't think of anything I'd rather do than walk both my beautiful daughters down the aisle on their wedding day. And from what I've seen, you're both getting great guys."

"Thanks, Daddy," Emma said. "We kind of like them."

The four young adults whispered among themselves for a minute, then Emma took the lead in the conversation.

"All four of us are in agreement that we want a fairly casual ceremony," Emma said. "Keeping that in mind, we've decided to make things easy on the guys. Well, except for the grooms. All the men in the wedding party will be wearing navy blue slacks and matching vests, along with a dusty blue tie."

"What about me?" Aaron asked.

"You're one of the men, Aaron," Emma replied with a smile. "So, naturally you will also be wearing navy blue slacks and a matching vest, with a dusty blue tie."

Aaron smiled widely and gave his dad a high-five.

"For the grooms," Emma continued, as she reached for Matt's hand, "Matt will wear a navy blue suit and vest, and a dusty blue tie. Aiden will be wearing his Class A uniform, the dress blues. For the ladies in the wedding party, depending on what we find, Sophie can wear either a dusty blue dress or a dress with a white bodice and dusty blue skirt. We'd like the matrons of honor to wear navy blue dresses and the moms to wear dusty blue dresses."

"I think those are the major decisions we have nailed down," Bailey added. "Then, of course, we'll have to make a trip to Seattle to go shopping for dresses!"

Spencer laughed from across the room. "Aiden, you and Matt are going to enjoy that trip!"

"Oh, no, they won't!" Bailey said. "The guys will not be allowed on that trip. They can't see the wedding dresses before the wedding. That will be an outing for just us girls."

"Saved by a technicality, guys," Wyatt said, chuckling. Then he and Spencer gave each other a high-five.

Todd chuckled at the antics of the girls' twin brothers. "I think we should be able to find the clothes for the guys right here locally. Or at least within fifty miles or so. Even Matt's suit shouldn't be a problem."

With the major decisions out of the way, the younger guys escaped to the family room to play video games, and the women huddled around the dining room table to plan a trip to Seattle.

* * *

A couple weeks later, Amy and little Levi joined Meghan and Sophie in Meghan's SUV for the trip to Seattle. Not long after they'd gotten Levi settled into his car seat, Bailey pulled into the driveway with Emma, Nicole, and Vicki. They had planned to get an early start so they could shop for all the dresses and still have time to shop for wedding bands for Aiden and Matt.

Once they arrived in Seattle, they picked up Hannah and headed into town to begin shopping. Their appointment at the bridal shop was first since they knew that would take the most time. Bailey and Emma knew they didn't want wedding dresses that were too frilly. That just wasn't their style. Nor did they want identical dresses. While they were browsing the wedding dresses with their mother, the other ladies headed toward a section of blue dresses.

Meghan had found several navy blue dresses, while Nicole

and Vicki found what they thought might be considered dusty blue dresses. After taking a dress of each color over to the girls to confirm color choices, they continued browsing the dresses to find their sizes in a couple of styles they all liked. Amy handed Levi off to Grandma Vicki while she tried on her dress and settled on one nearly identical to Meghan's. Amazed that none of their dresses would require alterations, the ladies paid for their purchases and had the dresses bagged up.

Bailey and Emma each found two dress styles they liked and were trying them on in the dressing rooms. That gave their mother time to look for a dress for herself. She loved the style of dress Vicki chose and was able to quickly find it in her size.

By the time the future brides had been helped into their first dresses and were both standing in front of the mirrors, the other ladies had gathered around to offer assistance. Two bridal attendants were pinning up the gowns while everyone admired their dress choices. Once the dresses were properly pinned, the girls stepped back to be able to see them from all angles in the mirrors.

"Oh, Bailey!" Emma said, looking over at her sister. "I love it! Your dress is beautiful! It's perfect for you. Do you like it?"

"This was my first choice," Bailey said beaming. "I was hoping I wouldn't even have to try on the second dress. I love this one. Do you really think it looks okay on me?"

"Yes!" Emma said emphatically. "You're beautiful, Bales. As long as you like it, I think that's the dress for you. I really do. What about my dress? What do you think of it?"

Bailey looked at her younger sister with love. "Emma, I honestly don't think either of us need to bother trying on another dress. It just screams 'you.' You're beautiful, and that dress looks perfect on you."

Both girls turned to the other women. "What do you ladies

think?" Bailey asked, looking right at her mother.

Hannah was standing with her hands covering her mouth and tears forming in her eyes. "I have the most beautiful daughters. Those dresses are perfect for both of you."

The other ladies walked up on the platform and walked around the girls, looking at the dresses from all angles. They were all wearing big smiles.

"I agree with your mother, girls," Meghan said. "Both dresses are beautiful."

Vicki and Nicole nodded their heads in agreement. "I don't think you have to look any further," Vicki said.

Amy had been standing back, holding Levi, and simply watching. "This all reminds me of my wedding not that long ago. Both guys will be blown away. You're gorgeous."

About that time, Sophie walked up and tapped Meghan on the arm. "Grandma," she said hesitantly. "What about me? I'm supposed to get a flower girl dress, right?"

"Oh!" Meghan said in surprise. "Sweetie, I'm so sorry! We got busy finding all our dresses and looking at Bailey and Emma's dresses. I forgot we still need to find you a dress. I'm sorry, honey. Let's go do that right this minute."

Sophie took her grandma's hand and walked toward the flower girl dresses, followed closely by the other women.

"I think we need to find you a very special dress, Sophie," Nicole said. "You've been so patient."

Finding several dresses in the right color, Meghan picked out Sophie's size and held it up to her. "Do you like this dress, Sophie?"

"Can I try it on Grandma, like you all did?"

"Oh, absolutely!" Meghan replied with a smile.

A few minutes later, Sophie was modeling the dress for the ladies in her family. She spun around several times, smiling at herself in the mirror.

"Can I get this one, Grandma?" Sophie asked hopefully. "I just love the way it twirls when I spin around."

"Oh, twirling is very important, Sophie," Vicki agreed seriously.

All the women nodded and agreed it was the perfect dress. A very happy Sophie returned to the dressing room to carefully change out of her new dress.

After gathering all their dress purchases and securing a date to return to try on wedding dresses after the alterations had been completed, everyone decided it was time to grab a quick bite of lunch before shopping for rings.

* * *

Once in the jewelry store, everyone walked toward the display cases containing men's wedding bands and began to get a general feel for what they wanted. Bailey and Emma asked Nicole and Vicki if they knew of any ring preferences their sons might have. Both women chuckled and said their sons didn't discuss jewelry with them.

After discussing a few different ideas, Bailey turned to her sister and said, "Okay, Emma, let's think about this for a minute. Both boys work in construction. They aren't going to want fancy wedding rings with diamonds that they have to take off every day when they go to work, right?"

"That's a good point, Bales," Emma said, nodding her head. "So, we probably want to find fairly basic rings. Do you think silver, to match the color of our rings?"

"I think that would probably look best," Bailey agreed.

After looking at a few rings in the display case and referring to the ring sizes they had saved in their phones, the girls asked the clerk to show them several different wedding bands.

Pulling out a tray of rings, the clerk said, "I heard you mention that your fiancés are in construction. I'd recommend one of these options made of tungsten. They're virtually scratchproof, and three times as strong as gold. Great for those who work with their hands."

"Oh, that's a great idea. We don't want them to have matching rings, though," Emma said. "That would be weird."

"I agree," Bailey said, chuckling. "I think Aiden would like this ring," she said, holding up a silver band with a matte finish. "It's not too fancy but isn't just plain either."

Holding up a silver band, also with a matte finish, Emma showed it to her sister. "What do you think of this ring? It's not the same as Aiden's. It has some subtle engraving on it. Do you think Matt would like it?"

Bailey took the ring, turning it over in her hand, then smiled. "I could see Matt liking this. I think it's perfect for him."

Satisfied with their choices, the girls asked the clerk if the rings were available in the necessary sizes. A few minutes later, he returned from the back room carrying two small ring boxes.

By the time the girls paid for the rings, it was midafternoon.

Bailey looked at the rest of the group as they stood in the lobby of the jewelry store. "We should probably take Mom back home, then hit the road."

"I agree," Meghan said. "I'm glad I put a pot roast in the crockpot this morning. Dinner will be ready by the time we get home."

Nicole chuckled and said, "Assuming the boys didn't figure that out and get to it before we do!"

Chapter Twenty-Three

Aiden and Matt had been staying in close contact with Roger and Mike so they would be ready to begin construction of the second house in the Hope Estates development as soon as Roger made a few last-minute decisions. As they pulled up along the curb in front of the completed first house, they saw Roger and Mike sitting in their pickup in the driveway.

The four men climbed out of their trucks and met on the sidewalk.

"Let's take a walk down to the corner," Roger suggested after shaking hands with the young men. "That corner lot is a little bigger than some of the others, and I think that's where we'll build the second house."

As they approached the corner lot, Mike pointed toward the center of the lot and said, "As you can see, the location for the house is already staked out. You boys should be able to start digging for the footings whenever you're ready."

Walking onto the lot and looking around, Matt said, "I assume those taller stakes mark the corners of the various lots."

"You're right, Matt," Roger confirmed.

"I realize things are going to be picking up at the construction company pretty soon," Roger said, "and you boys will be busy juggling things. I'm confident you will do just fine, but please let me know if you run into any problems."

"In the next few days," Mike began, "we'll have a map of the development. That way we can show you which lots we plan to build on next. Roger and I have talked about it, and we're pretty sure you can handle working on two houses in a piggyback fashion. Meaning, that when you finish digging the footings for this first house, you can move that equipment over and dig the footings for the next house. The same would go for pouring foundations, laying the subfloors, and framing. Pretty much all aspects of the building. All the way down to the painting. How are you guys set for crews?"

Aiden looked at Matt and turned back to reply. "We've already talked to Dad and Uncle Travis about the crews. We plan to use most of our original crew to work on the commercial projects. We've been pretty satisfied with the additional crews we picked up to work on your first house. It was nice to be able to keep most of them employed over the winter. Dad told us housing developments typically worked the way you were just discussing, which makes sense. So, I'm sure we'll be able to move crews back and forth between a couple of houses."

"Do you know when you'll stake out the location for the house after this one on the corner lot?" Matt asked. "It would make things easier if they were fairly close to each other."

"We'll do that in the next couple of days, Matt," Roger answered. "And you're correct. We do plan to have it close to this house. Very likely it won't be more than a lot or two away from this corner lot."

"Well, boys," Mike began, "Roger and I have a meeting to go to. We'll touch base with you again in a couple days. In the meantime, you can begin digging footings at this first house as soon as you can work it into your schedule."

Aiden and Matt walked back and climbed into their Byers Construction truck. Aiden turned to face Matt and said, "Two houses at once. Out of the frying pan and into the fire!"

"It sure looks like it," Matt said with a grin.

"I think it's time to make your dad a crew foreman," Aiden suggested. "I think he's ready. And we're going to need all the help we can get to keep crews organized and productive."

Matt nodded. "He would really like that. And we obviously still have Todd and Travis working as crew foreman too. I know they would kind of keep an eye on things. And, of course, you and I will be over here working part of the time as well."

Matt suddenly shook his head and laughed. "Boy, when we get busy, we really get busy!"

"That's a fact!" Aiden agreed with a laugh. "Hey, let's get some business cards made up for your dad, so we have those to give him when we tell him about his promotion."

"My dad is doing well enough at a job to get a promotion," Matt said as he shook his head in wonder. "I never would have believed that a few years ago."

* * *

Less than a week later, John pulled into the parking lot at Byers Construction and sat in his pickup. Matt had asked him to stop by the office before going over to the job site. He said they needed to talk. John had been wracking his brain, trying to figure out what he had done wrong that would require a meeting at the office. He hadn't been able to come up with a single thing. He was sure he'd been doing everything asked of him, and he thought he was doing a good job. He shook his head, climbed out of the truck, and slowly walked into the building.

"Hey, Steve," he addressed the man at the front counter. "Is

Matt around? I was supposed to meet him here."

"Hi, John," Steve replied. "He's back in the office. You can go on back."

"Okay," John replied quietly. "Thanks."

John knocked softly on the partly open office door.

"Come on in," someone answered from inside the room. John thought that sounded like Todd's voice.

John walked into the office and saw Todd, Travis, Aiden, and Matt all sitting around the small conference table.

"Come on in and grab a seat, Dad," Matt said, gesturing to an empty chair.

John took a seat, then looked around the table at the others. "So, what's up?"

"First of all, Dad," Matt began, "we want to thank you for helping out on Roger's house."

Completely confused and afraid he would say the wrong thing, John remained silent.

"We met with Roger and Mike a few days ago," Matt continued. "They've staked out the location for the third house in the development. As you know, we just started on the second one, but we'll be kind of building two houses at the same time. We'll sure be busy, but I think it'll be just fine."

Sliding a small box across the table to his dad, Matt said, "We have a little something for you."

When John made no move to take the box, Todd said, "Go ahead, John. Open it."

John looked around the table at the four men, pulled the box toward him, and opened it. Reaching inside the box, he removed a business card that looked just like the card Matt had shown him not long ago.

"Go ahead, Dad," Matt urged. "Read the card."

John looked at his son, then began to read the card. "Phoenix

Rising Homes, a subsidiary of Byers Construction. John Phoenix, Crew Foreman." John sat back in his chair, then looked over at his son. "Crew foreman? Really?"

Matt smiled, along with the other three men around the table. "Yes, Dad, crew foreman. You are officially being promoted!"

A grin slowly crept across John's face, quickly turning into a wide smile. "A promotion? To crew foreman? Seriously?"

Todd chuckled and said, "Yes, John. Seriously. We're about to get very busy, and we're going to need your help. You kind of got your feet wet helping out on JC and Amy's house, and then you learned a lot more on that first house in the development. The truth of the matter, John, is that you're a hard worker and a quick learner. We all think you would make a great crew foreman."

"Crew foreman," John said, shaking his head in disbelief. Suddenly, he stood up and pushed back his chair. "If I'm a foreman now, then I'd better quit sitting around here talking and get over to the job site and get to work!"

Before leaving the office, John shook hands with Todd, Travis, and Aiden, then gave Matt a big hug. "You guys won't regret it. I promise!"

Then he was out the door, leaving the others standing in the office smiling.

* * *

Spring was always a busy time of year in the construction industry, and that was certainly the case for Byers Construction this year. They had secured a couple of large commercial projects, in addition to several smaller projects. Adding the home building arm to the business meant they were even busier than normal. They had retained the extra laborers they hired to help with the first home in the Hope Estates development and had hired additional workers as well. Todd told Aiden and Matt to count on being incredibly busy for at least the next couple of years. Being hired as the general contractor for Hope Estates, whether it ended up being one phase or two, meant they would be building several houses. Byers Construction was growing beyond the family's wildest expectations.

Aiden and Matt had been juggling crews all spring as construction continued on the two houses in the development. With help from Travis and Todd, they were becoming experts at managing crews and knowing when to bring in subcontractors. Promoting John to crew foreman had been a smart move. He seemed to be a natural. All the workers liked him, and he enjoyed working right alongside everyone else.

Matt had been so busy handling the logistics of scheduling crews and subcontractors that he was beginning to miss doing the actual construction. When Todd pulled his truck alongside the curb in front of the corner house, he noticed Matt's Ford Ranger parked in the driveway. Todd grabbed his hard hat and toolbelt and walked in the front door. Looking around, he found Matt hanging drywall with his dad.

Todd smiled and walked over to the two men. He tapped Matt on the back and said, "So, you really do miss the down-and-dirty work, huh?"

Matt stopped what he was doing and smiled. "Yeah, I really do. I like doing the actual building."

"You know, Matt," Todd said as he spoke from years of experience, "you can find a balance. I was the same way when I took over the company. I found myself spending more time running the business and less time doing the actual construction. I was becoming unhappy... until I decided to do something about it. You don't have to let that happen to you. You're young. You have a lot of energy. There's no reason you can't spend part of your time scheduling workers and part of your time working on the houses."

"You think so?" Matt asked, unsure of himself.

Todd grinned. "Matt, between you and Aiden, you guys schedule all the crews. Nothing is stopping you from scheduling yourself on one of the crews."

Matt grinned. "You're right. I guess I never thought about that because it's been so busy."

Todd patted Matt on the back and said, "Make sure you can always see the trees through the forest, Matt. Don't be so blinded by the big picture that you miss out on the little things." Looking over at John, Todd added, "Now, you'd better get back to work. It looks to me like your crew foreman wants to hang some more drywall."

* * *

Construction on the two homes continued throughout the spring as the next two houses were added to their lineup. Matt and Aiden had both been able to find a balance between running Byers Construction and keeping the commercial projects on time, continuing to build houses in the development, and finding time to do some of the hands-on construction work. Of course, the dilemma of when they would have time to build their own homes was always in the back of their minds.

During one of the many family dinners at Travis and Meghan's house, that was a topic of discussion. Bailey and Aiden were sitting across the table from Matt and Emma after dinner. The four young adults were lamenting the fact that although they had been able to decide on some of the features they wanted for each of their homes, they simply had not had the time to do anything beyond that.

Meghan looked over at Travis and smiled. Turning to the young adults at the table, she said, "Travis and I have been tossing around an idea that might help, if you're agreeable to it."

"What have you been thinking about?" Bailey asked.

"If you kids would like, I'd be more than happy to do the design of both your homes," Meghan said. "We could sit down at some point, and you could tell me what you have in mind, a basic floor plan, what specific features you would like, and we could brainstorm. I don't want you to feel pressured to allow me to do the design work, but I would love to do it for you."

The four young adults looked at each other, then they all smiled.

"Aunt Meghan," Aiden began, "we would love to have you design our homes. We've all talked about how much we like the look of this house and the home you helped design for JC and Amy. You do great work, and you have so many fantastic ideas. We just didn't want to put that burden on you because we know you guys have been working toward retirement."

"I assure you," Meghan said sincerely, "it is no burden at all. In fact, I want to do it as a wedding gift to you kids."

"Are you sure, Meghan?" Bailey asked.

"Yes, I'm sure," Meghan replied. "Consider it a done deal. You kids can discuss what you want, then we can get together and hash out some details. Then you can leave the design work to me, and you can concentrate on your other responsibilities. You all have a lot on your plates right now."

"And we have a wedding coming up!" Matt said.

"That will be here before you know it," Travis said. "So, it's time to let us take some of the extra things off your plates."

With that, Matt shoved his empty dessert plate in Travis's direction. "Speaking of empty plates," Matt said with a grin, "any chance I can get a refill of that strawberry shortcake?"

Travis laughed as he took Matt's empty plate and headed to the kitchen.

Chapter Twenty-Four

The big wedding was now less than a month away. Bailey and Emma had gone back to Seattle for the final fitting of their wedding dresses, and they were safely stored at Meghan's house. Todd and Travis had spearheaded the effort to find matching slacks, vests, and ties for the guys in the wedding party, along with the suit for Matt. Aiden had taken his dress blues in to be freshly cleaned and now had them hanging in his closet. Things were beginning to come together. The only problem was trying to finish the second house in the development before the wedding.

Aiden and Matt wanted the second house to be completed before the wedding so they could take a short break for their honeymoon. For a while, it didn't look like that would happen. They kept encountering delays in receiving materials, and that had put them a bit behind. The construction of the third house was just far enough behind the second one that the material delays didn't affect it. Once the delayed materials had finally arrived, the guys pulled crews off the third house, so they had everyone working to complete house number two. Juggling workers had become a challenge, but they were making it work.

Finally, with the wedding just a little over two weeks away, Matt and Aiden were doing a final walk-through of the second house before bringing Roger and Mike in to sign off on it. Travis and Todd had already gone through the house earlier, and they hadn't found anything that needed attention.

Hearing a truck door close out front, Matt looked out the living room window and saw Roger and Mike climbing out of their R & M Development pickup.

"Aiden," Matt called into the other room, "Mike and Roger are here."

Aiden walked into the living room to join Matt. "I think we're ready for them."

Matt walked over and opened the front door before the men had a chance to ring the doorbell.

"Hey, Mike," Matt said, shaking Mike's hand. He then shook Roger's hand and said, "Come on in. We think we're ready for you guys to look over the house."

Standing in the middle of the living room, Roger glanced around, nodding his head in satisfaction.

"I was sure you boys would be able to get this one finished before your wedding," Roger said. Then he chuckled as he added, "It was touch and go there for a bit with those unexpected material delays."

Aiden laughed and said, "Yeah, I think we both aged a bit waiting for things to arrive!"

Roger smiled as he said, "Welcome to the world of home construction. But you boys really impressed us. You didn't waste any time sitting around waiting for materials to arrive. You pulled your crew off this house and moved it over to the third one and kept working. You hardly missed a beat."

"It sure didn't feel that easy from our end," Aiden said. "We were sweating it there for a while. We're just glad things started arriving when they did."

Roger had a small notebook in his hand as he walked toward

the far end of the house. Looking at Mike, he said, "Why don't we start back in the bedrooms and work our way to the other end of the house?"

"Sounds good to me," Mike agreed, as the two men headed toward the bedrooms.

"We'll get out of your way," Matt said. "We'll be out front when you're finished. Just let us know if you need us for anything."

Matt and Aiden walked out to the pickup, lowered the tailgate, and sat down to wait. They waited in silence. Even though they had been through this process once before, on the first house, it was still a little nerve-wracking. And, of course, in the back of both their minds was the question of having to make repairs or changes with the wedding fast approaching.

Half an hour later, Roger and Mike came out the front door, closed it behind them, and walked over to the young men. The young contractors hopped off the tailgate of their pickup and met the older men in the driveway.

The two older men tried to keep poker faces, but they failed. They both broke out in smiles as they reached out to shake Aiden and Matt's hands.

"You know, boys," Roger began, "I told Mike at the beginning that I thought you two had a bright future ahead of you building houses. You've proven me right. We didn't find a single thing wrong. You've done a great job, and you should be proud of yourselves. Phoenix Rising Homes is here to stay."

Matt and Aiden smiled and shook each other's hands.

"Did you hear that, Matt?" Aiden asked, wearing a huge grin. "Phoenix Rising Homes is here to stay."

Matt grinned and replied, "Wow. A few years ago, I never could've imagined this. But here we are, building houses."

"Now, I realize you boys probably want to be able to catch

your breath a bit before the wedding," Roger said. "But I do have one other thing I'd like you to do for me if you would."

"Whatever you need, Roger," Aiden replied.

"Do you think you can meet me and Mike back over here tomorrow afternoon?" Roger asked. "And bring Todd, Travis, and John along with you. We'd like to talk to you guys."

"My dad?" Matt asked with curiosity.

"Yes," Roger confirmed. "How about we all meet up here about one-thirty tomorrow afternoon?"

Aiden and Matt looked at each other in confusion, then Matt replied, "Not a problem. We'll be here."

With that, they all shook hands, then the older men climbed into their pickup and drove away.

"What do you think that's all about?" Matt asked Aiden as they went back to lock up the house.

"Boy, I don't have a clue. There can't be anything wrong with the house," Aiden said, pointing to a piece of paper sitting on the kitchen counter. "They signed off on it."

* * *

By one-fifteen the next afternoon, Matt was pacing on the front porch of the finished house. Todd and Aiden were leaning against the Byers Construction pickup parked in the driveway. Travis and John were walking up and down the sidewalk along the street. They were all anxiously awaiting the arrival of the now-familiar R & M Development pickup. Aiden and Matt had talked to Todd and Travis about the meeting, but neither of them had any idea what it was about. So, they waited.

Just before one-thirty, Aiden pointed to the R & M Development pickup coming down the street. After parking the truck in the driveway, Roger and Mike climbed out and greeted the other men.

Pulling the house key out of his pocket, Roger said, "Let's all go inside so we can talk."

Shrugging their shoulders, Matt and Aiden joined Roger and Mike on the front porch. They were followed by Todd, Travis, and John, all equally confused.

Once they were all gathered in the middle of the living room, Roger looked around the group and smiled.

"I see a lot of confused looks," Roger said with a chuckle. "Well, I'll clear everything up in a minute.

"First of all," Roger continued, "Mike and I want to tell you older guys how impressed we are with Aiden and Matt. I have to admit when Mike first mentioned the idea of giving the boys a chance, I wasn't too keen on the idea. Then again, Mike has always been a better judge of character than I am. But I know when to trust my gut instincts and when to listen to my partner. I'm glad I did both where the boys are concerned. I've always liked being able to give start-up companies a chance, especially when they're being run by young people. And I've always liked giving people a second chance in life when they've maybe been knocked around a bit.

"When I saw that first house you boys built for JC and Amy," Roger continued, "I was surprised. Very surprised. Mike and I both saw your potential. The first house you built for us impressed me even further. By then, I was convinced you had a great future ahead of you. Now, you've finished this second house for us, with the third one not far behind."

Looking at John, Roger said, "John, why don't you come over here and stand beside me for a minute?"

John, still as confused as the others, looked at his son, then at Travis, who simply shrugged.

John was hesitant but did as he was asked and walked over

to stand beside Roger.

Roger shook John's hand and smiled. "John," Roger began, "I know you had a hand in building that first house for your daughter."

Sensing his discomfort, Roger put his hand on John's shoulder before continuing.

"I also know there was an issue with that house," Roger said. "But I heard about the hard work you put in to try to correct your mistake. It takes a big man to do what you did. Mike and I watched you work right alongside the others building that first house in our development. You worked hard, and you learned quickly. When Phoenix Rising Homes was signed on as the general contractor for the development, Aiden and Matt made a wise decision when they promoted you to crew foreman.

"You were one of the crew foremen on this second house," Roger continued. "You have a lot of sweat equity in this house, and we can tell you take pride in your work."

Roger reached into his pocket and pulled out a house key on a chain.

Holding the key out to John, he said, "Because we like being able to give people a second chance when they've earned it, and you have certainly earned it, Mike and I have decided to gift this house to you and your wife."

"What?" John asked, clearly confused.

Mike walked over and stood on the other side of John. "Roger and I are giving you and Vicki this house, John. I know you've had a lot of rough years. I also know it was because of your own choices. But *you* made the choice to turn your life around. You've worked hard, very hard, and you've earned the right to start over with a clean slate."

John shook his head. "We don't need charity, Mike."

Mike turned so he was looking John square in the face. "This is not charity, John. As Roger said, you have a lot of sweat equity in this house. It's not charity. You've earned it. And we want you to have it."

As tears welled up in the corners of his eyes, John still made no attempt to take the key from Roger's hand.

"Take the key, John," Mike said.

Matt walked up to his dad and looked him in the eye. Reaching over and taking the key from Roger's still outstretched hand, Matt placed the key in his dad's hand and closed his fingers around it.

"Take the key, Dad," Matt said, with tears in his eyes. "They want you to have it. You've earned it. I'm proud of you, Dad."

John broke down in tears and wrapped his arms around his son. After a couple minutes, he pulled away and walked over to sit on the floor against the living room wall.

"I need to sit down before I fall down!" John said with a small chuckle.

Matt sat down on the floor beside his dad, then all the other men joined them and formed a circle sitting on the living room floor.

John looked around the circle at everyone. Obviously still very emotional, he said, "I don't even know what to say. You have no idea what this means to me. What it will mean to my wife when I tell her! Matt, you may have to come home with me to tell your mom. She's never going to believe me!"

All the men chuckled as John sat on the floor, shaking his head in disbelief.

Then he held up the key to his new home and said, "To second chances! God is good!"

To which Travis added, "All the time!"

Chapter Twenty-Five

Two days before the wedding, the Campbell family arrived in Hope. Since Ryleigh was also in town for the wedding, Joseph Campbell insisted his sons stay with them at the Hope Inn, rather than infringing on space at the Harmon home. Although, in reality, everyone spent most of their time at Travis and Meghan's home anyway. Hannah understandably wanted to be available to help her daughters with any last-minute needs they might have, as well as to help calm their nerves.

Kaci and Ryleigh were spearheading a big spaghetti dinner for the entire family the first night the Campbells were in town. That freed up Meghan to help the other ladies with some of the final details. The rehearsal was scheduled for early afternoon the day before the wedding, followed by a rehearsal dinner that evening, which Mike Slater had insisted he was sponsoring. Reservations were made at the nicest restaurant in Hope, where they would all gather shortly after the rehearsal.

When everyone arrived at Hope Community Church for the afternoon rehearsal, the church was completely decorated for the wedding. Dusty blue and white flowers, tied with navy blue ribbons, decorated the pews as well as several standing baskets up front. The decorations were perfect for the four young adults –

nothing was overly elaborate. Everything about the setup in the sanctuary spoke to the personalities of the two young couples.

The rehearsal went off without a hitch. Everyone, including the "experienced" flower girl and ring bearer, seemed to know their responsibilities. There was a lot of laughter throughout the rehearsal, which did its intended job of easing pre-wedding jitters. After the first run-through, Aaron and Sophie made another theatrical skip down the aisle, scattering imaginary flowers in all directions. Not to be outdone by the kids, Wyatt and Spencer followed them down the aisle, also skipping and scattering imaginary flowers. The adults standing at the pulpit couldn't contain their laughter.

At one point, Hannah looked at her twin sons and smiled. "You boys do remember you're twenty-four, right? Maybe you should consider acting your age."

"I don't know, Mom," Emma said, looking at her brothers. "That actually looks like fun. Besides, tomorrow we'll all be old married people. Today is our last day of being kids."

With that, Emma grabbed her sister by the hand and happily skipped back down the aisle. Matt looked over at Aiden, and they both shrugged, joined hands, and followed their future brides, skipping down the aisle and out the door.

* * *

Everyone enjoyed a fantastic meal at the rehearsal dinner. Mike had requested a buffet that had every kind of food a person could want. Several types of meat, seafood, pasta dishes, salads, desserts, and bread filled the table, which was decorated in the navy, dusty blue and white colors of the wedding party.

As the meal was winding down, people settled back to regroup and discuss any last-minute details that may need to be handled.

"You know," Bailey said, "as soon as we return from the honeymoon, at least two of us are going to have to pack up and move. I need to move over to Aiden's apartment."

"And I need to move back over to your apartment with Emma," Matt said, laughing. "It seems strange that I'll be moving back to the same apartment where I lived with my sister."

"If you kids are okay with it," Todd began, "we could get your things moved while you're away on your honeymoon. I don't know about Bailey, but it won't take long to move Matt's things."

Bailey and Matt looked at their future spouses and shrugged. "I certainly don't have a problem with it," Bailey said.

"Me neither," Matt said in agreement. "It's one less thing we have to do when we get back. We're going to be plenty busy with those next two houses in the development and figuring out when we can start building our own homes."

"It will be nice to come back and just settle into our new places," Bailey said. "Thank you."

Looking at the soon-to-be-married couples, Meghan asked, "Are you spending your entire honeymoon in Victoria, B.C.? Or do you plan to explore more of British Columbia?"

"There's plenty to see and do in Victoria," Aiden answered. "So, we plan to stay there. We can always go back another time."

"You'll love Victoria," Travis added. "It's a beautiful city and, you're right, there are a lot of things to do there."

"We'll be nearby in Vancouver. Close enough to caravan, far enough to do our own thing," Matt added, taking Emma's hand.

Reaching for his wife's hand, Joseph said, "Hannah and I went to Vancouver not long after we were married. We always wanted to go back to see Victoria, but we haven't made it yet. Maybe someday."

"You know," Meghan said, "maybe one of these days we could all take a big family vacation to B.C.! That would be a lot of fun!"

"That does sound fun," Aiden yawned as he pushed back his chair. "I don't know about everyone else, but I'm beat. And we have a wedding tomorrow, followed by a trip to Canada the next day. So, I think I'm ready to call it a day."

Bailey stood and took Aiden's hand. "Me too. I suspect tomorrow will be a very busy day!"

* * *

One of the rooms at the church had been converted into a makeshift bridal room, and Travis had brought in three full-length mirrors for the brides to use in their preparations. Hannah and Amy were helping Bailey and Emma into their wedding gowns.

As the gowns were being fastened on each of the brides, Meghan looked over at the girls with a smile. "You know," she said with a chuckle, "when I was getting dressed before my wedding, my best friend walked in to tell me the limo had arrived. She looked down at my feet, lifted the hem of my dress, and laughed."

Emma smiled in curiosity. "Why did she laugh?"

Meghan laughed at the memory. "I got married in my best cowboy boots!"

"You didn't!" Bailey said, laughing.

"Yep," Meghan confirmed. "I most certainly did. Travis was so jealous because he didn't think he could get away with wearing his boots, so he didn't even try!"

Kaci had been sitting in a chair in the corner of the room, holding a squirming ten-month-old Levi so his mom could help Emma.

"She is absolutely telling the truth," Kaci assured the other brides. "It was all I could do to convince her to wear a wedding dress. She wanted to get married in her Levis! The boots were a compromise!"

All the women in the room burst out laughing as they continued with their preparations. Before long, both brides were fully dressed and standing in front of the mirrors.

Hannah stepped back and looked at her two daughters. "You two are beautiful," she said in a near whisper. "I would wrap you both in a hug, but I don't want to mess anything up."

"That's okay, Mom," Bailey said. "There will be plenty of time for hugging after the ceremony."

"And pictures!" Emma added. "Don't forget we're having pictures taken before the reception."

Meghan and Amy reached onto the table to retrieve the two bridal veils. Meghan carefully positioned Bailey's veil on her head, and Amy did the same for Emma. Then Hannah walked over to her daughters and very carefully clipped a small blue rose into Bailey's dark hair and clipped a matching rose into Emma's long blonde hair.

The two brides were beautiful.

Hannah gave each of her daughters a very careful hug, then said, "I guess it's time. We'll see you out in the lobby in a few minutes."

A short time later, the entire wedding party, along with both brides, met in the lobby just outside the sanctuary. Playing over the speakers was the special music the four had selected for the wedding.

The brides' attendants were careful to keep the brides away from the windows so the grooms wouldn't see them until they walked down the aisle. When they received the signal, the doors to the sanctuary were opened for the wedding party, and the brides stepped back away from the doors.

Aiden and Bailey's attendants were to be first, followed by Matt and Emma's attendants. Todd took his sister Meghan's hand, tucked it into the crook of his arm, and took their place at the head of the line. John took Amy's hand and tucked it into the crook of his arm, falling in line behind Todd and Meghan.

Travis was standing in front of the pulpit, his Bible in his hand. The two grooms were standing at the head of the aisle, anxiously awaiting their brides. When Travis gave a slight nod of his head, Todd and Meghan started down the aisle, followed by John and Amy. The mothers of the grooms, Nicole and Vicki, came next. Lastly, Hannah walked up the aisle, flanked by her twin sons.

At another nod from Travis, Sophie with her basket of flower petals, and Aaron with his ring pillow, started up the aisle. Both kids took their roles very seriously. They were professionals, after all! Sophie scattered flower petals while smiling and making eye contact with many of the guests. Aaron stared straight ahead, clutching the pillow in his hands, his eyes glued on his papa standing in front of the pulpit.

Once the flower girl and ring bearer completed their duties, the doors to the sanctuary opened once again, and the wedding march began to play.

Joseph Campbell took the hand of his oldest daughter and tucked it safely into the crook of his right arm. He then took his youngest daughter's hand and tucked it into the crook of his left arm.

Smiling at his two beautiful little girls, who weren't so little anymore, he said, "I love you both more than life itself." Then he stood straight and proud and began walking them down the aisle.

As they walked toward the front of the church, Bailey marveled at how handsome Aiden looked in his Class A dress blues. She smiled widely as she walked down the aisle on her father's arm. Emma was equally impressed by Matt in his sharp navy blue suit.

At the front of the church, Aiden and Matt's eyes were transfixed on their gorgeous brides walking up the aisle on their father's arms. The two young men looked at each other and smiled.

Reaching the front of the church, Joseph handed Bailey over to Aiden, then handed Emma over to Matt, giving each of his daughters a kiss on the cheek.

Once everyone was seated, Travis addressed the guests.

"As you all know," Travis began, "this is a very special day. We have gathered here to unite Aiden and Bailey, and Matt and Emma, in holy matrimony. I am honored to be able to perform the ceremony for these fine young adults whom I consider family."

He then glanced at Aiden and said with a smile, "Well, actually one truly is family. But I claim the other three, too."

Travis went on to give the young couples some fatherly advice and also reminded them of the importance of keeping God at the center of their marriages.

"I truly believe these four young people were brought together by God," Travis said. "Some would say it was simply circumstances or a series of coincidences. I know that's not the case. These four are together because they are meant to be.

"The kids have written their own vows," Travis began before chuckling. "I really need to stop referring to them as kids. They're getting married in a few minutes. They aren't kids anymore."

Everyone chuckled as several parents in the sanctuary nodded their heads in understanding.

"We're going to start with Aiden and Bailey," Travis said. Turning to Bailey, he said, "Bailey, go ahead."

Bailey reached out and took both of Aiden's hands in her

own, looking into his eyes. "Aiden, the first time I met you on that Army base a million miles away, I knew you were special. Your good heart couldn't help but shine through whenever you were around people. Your friends could see it, your fellow soldiers could see it, and I could see it. I felt so honored to be your friend while we were in the Army. I had no idea our paths would cross again two years later. And even in my wildest dreams, I never thought I would be the woman lucky enough to get to be your wife. But, here we are. I love you, Aiden. And I can't wait to begin our lives together."

Turning to his nephew, Travis said, "Go ahead, Aiden."

Looking into Bailey's eyes, Aiden began. "Bailey, my heart pales next to yours. Helping people is at the core of your being. Going into the ministry was the best choice you could have made. Your heart hurts whenever anyone around you is hurting. You live to help people and make their lives better. When I saw you coming out of this very church after your job interview, you literally took my breath away. I never thought I would see you again after the Army. I have no doubt God brought you here to Hope because we're meant to be together. I will spend the rest of my life trying to be the husband you deserve. I love you, Bailey."

Travis smiled, then turned his attention to the other couple.

"Now it's your turn," Travis said, looking at Matt and Emma. "Emma, you first."

Emma took Matt's hands in hers and smiled. "Well, shortstop, here we are."

Her nickname for him elicited a chuckle from Matt.

"There's no doubt I'm here because God sent me here," Emma began seriously. "I simply rode along with Bailey so she would have some company on the drive to her job interview. I fully expected to return to Seattle and spend the next several years working in some bland high-rise office building downtown. But

God knew I needed you. And He knew you needed me. You are amazing, Matt. You never see a roadblock or obstacle in front of you. All you see are challenges or mountains to conquer. Whatever you set your mind on doing, you just do it. We belong together, Matt." Then she added with a chuckle, "Of course, it helps that you like baseball. I love you, Matt, and I can't wait to build our dreams together."

Turning to Matt with a smile, Travis said, "Okay, Matt, it's your turn."

Matt smiled widely at Emma, then began, "Emma, nothing I say about you would come close to describing how special you are. You complete me. I could have wandered blindly through life without you and never knew what I was missing. But you're right. God knew I needed you. So, He brought you here to Hope so we could build a life together. I'm not amazing, Emma. I'm just plain old Matt. I'm only amazing when I'm the other half of you. We belong together, Emma. I love you more than you'll ever know."

Travis smiled as he looked at the two couples. "I love it when young people write their own vows. I could never come up with anything half as good as they just shared."

Turning toward his ever-vigilant grandson, Travis said, "Okay, Aaron, it's time to hand the rings over. You did a great job."

Making sure all parties had the proper rings, Travis turned to his nephew and said, "Aiden Leonard Byers, do you take this woman to be your lawfully wedded wife?"

"I do," Aiden replied, looking into Bailey's eyes.

Turning to Bailey, Travis asked, "Bailey Jo Campbell, do you take this man to be your lawfully wedded husband?"

"Yes, I do," Bailey replied.

Todd handed Aiden Bailey's ring.

"Aiden," Travis said, "place the ring on Bailey's finger and repeat after me. 'With this ring, I thee wed.'"

Aiden slid the ring onto Bailey's finger, squeezed her hand, and said, "With this ring, I thee wed."

Meghan then handed Aiden's ring to Bailey, and Travis said, "Bailey, place the ring on Aiden's finger and repeat after me. 'With this ring, I thee wed.'"

As Bailey slipped the ring onto Aiden's finger, she said, "With this ring, I thee wed."

Travis looked at the first couple and said, "I now pronounce you husband and wife." Then he added with a chuckle, "Now, hang on and don't go anywhere."

Travis then turned his attention to Matt and Emma.

"Matthew John Phoenix," Travis began, "do you take this woman to be your lawfully wedded wife?"

"Oh, yeah!" Matt replied with enthusiasm. "Uh, I mean, yes, I do."

Looking at Emma, Travis asked, "Emma Sloane Campbell, do you take this man to be your lawfully wedded husband?"

"I sure do!" Emma replied with a grin.

Chuckling, Travis turned to Matt while John handed Emma's ring to his son. "Matt, place the ring on Emma's finger and repeat after me. 'With this ring, I thee wed.'"

Matt slipped the ring onto Emma's finger, smiled, and said, "With this ring, I thee wed."

As Emma took Matt's ring from Amy, Travis said, "Emma, place the ring on Matt's finger and repeat after me. 'With this ring, I thee wed.'"

Emma looked at Matt, slid the ring onto his finger, then said, "With this ring, I thee wed."

Travis looked at the second couple and said, "I now pronounce you husband and wife."

Looking around, Travis asked with a laugh, "Did we get

everybody? Okay, gentlemen, you may now kiss your brides!"

Aiden and Matt both pulled their respective brides into their arms and gave them their first kisses as married women.

Placing a hand on Matt's back, Travis said to the couples, "Why don't the four of you turn to face the audience? Ladies and gentlemen, I proudly present to you Mr. and Mrs. Aiden Byers and Mr. and Mrs. Matthew Phoenix!"

The four young couples raised their hands in the air, then Aiden and Bailey started down the aisle, followed by Matt and Emma, Travis, then the rest of the wedding party.

* * *

Directly after the wedding, the photographer was taking candid shots as well as posed pictures of the new brides and grooms. Since Matt and Amy never had any family pictures while they were growing up, they wanted to make sure they got some at the wedding. The photographer took several nice shots of Matt with his parents, and Matt and Emma with his parents.

After getting a picture with his new wife and his parents, Matt called to Amy who was sitting a couple tables away, holding Levi.

"Amy," Matt said, "come over so I can get a picture of me and you with Dad and Mom. I also want a picture of me and Emma, you, JC, and Levi, and Mom and Dad."

Amy smiled as she handed her son to Josh, then walked over and stood beside her brother.

"I hope you know, Matt," Amy said, smiling, "I'm going to want copies of these pictures."

Vicki pulled her daughter in close and said, "Me too. It will be wonderful having a few nice pictures of my two kids."

Matt and Amy stood in the middle, with John standing beside his son and Vicki standing beside her daughter. They were all smiles in this first-ever family portrait.

After the formal photographs were taken, the young brides wanted to be sure they got pictures of them and their husbands cutting the wedding cake before they changed out of their bridal gowns. A table at the front of the church fellowship hall held a large wedding cake, along with several trays of cupcakes and chocolate chip cookies.

Once the cake-cutting pictures had been taken, the brides and grooms planned to escape to change into more comfortable clothing for the reception. As he started to walk away from the table, Matt asked, "Meghan, did you make these chocolate chip cookies?"

Meghan smiled and replied, "Yes, Matt, I did."

Matt grabbed two cookies, handed one to Aiden, then headed toward the changing room. He called back over his shoulder, "Make sure to save some of those cookies for me. I wouldn't want to starve at my own wedding!" Then he ran off, laughing.

It wasn't long before the newly married couples returned to the fellowship hall for the informal reception. Friends, family, and conversation filled the hall as they enjoyed a light dinner. Aiden, Bailey, Matt, and Emma sat down at a table with their parents. The Campbells were having a wonderful time getting to know the rest of the family better. A couple tables away, Wyatt and Spencer were laughing with JC, Amy, and Ryleigh, while little Levi was being happily passed from lap to lap.

When the dancing started, several couples took to the dance floor. Joseph and Hannah were dancing not far from their daughters, content to see how happy they were.

"You know, honey," Joseph said quietly to his wife, "the girls have married into a wonderful family. It's not easy having them a couple hours away, but there's no doubt they'll be taken care of and loved."

"I guess that just means we'll need to make more trips over the mountains," Hannah said with a contented smile.

Aiden and Bailey moved over so they were dancing beside Matt and Emma. They were looking around at the other couples on the dance floor.

"Your parents look happy, Matt," Aiden said nodding in John and Vicki's direction.

Looking toward his parents, Matt replied, "Yeah, they do. I don't think I've ever seen them truly happy before. It's kind of nice. A lot has changed in the past few years."

Aiden pulled his wife close and replied, "Yes, it has. God is good."

Still swaying with the music, Matt leaned down and kissed his wife. "All the time."

Epilogue

A Year Later

Aiden and Matt joined Todd, Travis, and John in the newly expanded conference room at Byers Construction. In the center of the conference table was a large map of the Hope Estates development. The men were looking at the map with satisfaction as they counted the number of red checkmarks that showed lots where houses had been completed by Phoenix Rising Homes. It had been a busy couple of years as the family business continued to grow, thanks in no small part to the addition of the home-building arm of the company.

Matt's dad, John Phoenix, had become such a valuable part of the construction team that he had been promoted once again. He was now a senior crew chief and supervised several of the crews who worked on building the homes.

Todd turned toward the open door when they heard a light knock on the door. Roger and Mike, from R & M Development, stood in the doorway.

"Come on in gentlemen," Todd said. "We've been waiting for you."

"I hope we didn't keep you guys waiting too long," Roger

said with a smile.

"Not at all," Aiden said, as he stood to shake hands with both men.

Mike looked at the map spread out on the conference table and nodded his head with satisfaction.

"That map has a lot of red checkmarks on it now," Mike said. "That means you boys have been busy!"

Matt chuckled as he replied, "Busy doesn't begin to cover it, Mike! These last two years have been insane! But it's been so much fun!"

Mike patted Matt on the back as he sat down beside him, chuckling as if he was keeping a secret.

Roger sat in another empty chair across the table from Mike. Looking over the map, he nodded his head. "There are only two lots on that map that don't have red checkmarks on them, and you boys are already working on those houses."

Looking up from the map, Roger addressed Aiden and Matt. "Do you have a timeframe on how long it will be before you finish those?"

Aiden looked at Matt before replying. "We were just talking about that the other day. As long as there aren't any more delays with materials, we should be able to wrap them up in a couple months. Does that sound right?"

"That seems doable to me," Matt said. Looking over at Todd and Travis, he asked, "What do you guys think?"

"I don't see why not," Todd agreed. "We have good solid crews working on the commercial projects, so there shouldn't be a reason to have to pull any of the guys off the houses to help elsewhere."

Mike glanced at Matt and Aiden and said, "I'm not sure how you boys have managed to find the time to build your own homes, but I bet it feels good to have them finished."

A big grin took over Matt's face as he replied, "I don't think I've ever done anything as satisfying in my life as building that house for me and Emma."

"I know what you mean, Matt," Aiden added. "Who would have thought a few years ago that we would have been building our own homes?"

Roger cleared his throat and said, "I'm glad you both have your homes finished. And, you're working on the final two homes in the development. That is, Phase One of the development."

Aiden and Matt looked at each other in confusion.

Roger smiled as he pulled something out of his pocket and spread what appeared to be another map out on the table.

Looking around the table at the other men, Roger said with a smile as he pointed to the new map. "Welcome to Phase Two of Hope Estates."

Matt looked at Aiden, then over to his dad, Todd, and Travis. "Phase Two?"

Mike laughed at the looks on the young men's faces. "Well, we wouldn't want you boys to get bored!"

"That should keep you two busy and out of trouble for the next couple of years!" Todd said with a chuckle.

Aiden reached over and gave Matt a high-five. "Phoenix Rising Homes is here to stay!"

* * *

Cars lined the driveways at Matt and Emma's house, Aiden and Bailey's house, and even spilled over to JC and Amy's house. There were lots of reasons to celebrate, and the family was having a large barbecue. The entire Harmon, Byers, Phoenix, and Campbell families had gathered in Matt and Emma's backyard. As was the case at nearly every family gathering, Mike Slater and his booming laugh were present. A badminton net had been set up next to a cornhole game, and everyone was having a great time.

Eleven-year-old twins Aaron and Sophie had abandoned their badminton rackets in favor of the cornhole game. They were whispering and giggling, then took off running for the back deck.

"Mr. Mike! Mr. Mike!" Sophie called as she ran up onto the deck. "Come play cornhole with me and Aaron."

Kaci laughed and said, "Kids, maybe Mr. Mike would like to relax and visit with the grownups."

"He can visit with the grownups anytime," Aaron said logically. "How often does he get a chance to play cornhole with me and Sophie?"

Mike laughed as he climbed out of his comfy deck chair and said, "You have a point there, Aaron. I don't know much about cornhole. Baseball is more my game, but let's go give it a try."

Sophie clapped her hands in excitement, then took Mike by the hand and led him to the backyard. "We can teach you, Mr. Mike. It'll be fun!"

Just as the older kids got to the cornhole board, Mike said, "It looks like we'll have to wait our turn."

Little Levi, just shy of his second birthday, had grabbed one of the bags for the game and was slowly walking up the board. When he got to the hole at the top of the board, he dropped the bag into the hole, then looked at his older cousins and began clapping.

"Good job, Levi!" Aaron said as he gave the little boy a high-five.

"See, Mr. Mike," Sophie said. "Even Levi can do it!"

Not far away, Spencer and Ryleigh had challenged Wyatt and Bailey to a game of badminton. As the game heated up, several of the other young adults gathered around to cheer on their favorite players. At one point, Spencer made a spectacular return hit that scored a point for him and Ryleigh.

Watching from the sidelines, Emma said with a chuckle, "Very impressive, Spence. When did you pull yourself away from the computer long enough to learn to play badminton?"

Spence just laughed as he teamed up with Ryleigh to return another volley. "I have a multi-faceted personality, sis. I have talents that would surprise you. I've even joined a bowling league!"

Then he returned another volley by hitting the birdie between his legs.

"Now you're just showing off!" Emma laughed.

Wyatt smashed a hard hit toward Spencer, who missed when he tried to hit the birdie from behind his back.

"Don't give up your day job, little brother!" Wyatt laughed.

Having fired up the grills, the older adults were laughing at the antics of the others playing games in the backyard. While Todd, Travis, and Jason grilled burgers, hotdogs, ribs, and corn on the cob, some of the others were filling tables along the back of the house with fruit, vegetables, salads, and other side dishes. Before long, the meat was being taken off the grills and placed on the tables.

From the back deck, Todd let out a shrill whistle to get everyone's attention. "It's time to eat! There's plenty of food, so don't trip anyone trying to get to the table!"

The games were abandoned in the yard as people ran for the back deck. On the way up the steps, Wyatt reached out and gave his brother a high-five. "Nice game, Spence. How about a one-on-one after dinner?"

"You're on, big brother," Spencer agreed as he handed his twin a plate and gestured for him to go ahead in line.

Once everyone had filled their plates and found a place to sit, Todd raised his hand to get everyone's attention.

"Does everyone have their plate filled for the first go-round?" Todd asked with a laugh. "Okay, perfect. Travis, would you mind blessing the food for us?"

"I would love to, Todd," Travis replied.

"Dear Heavenly Father," Travis began. "We come to you this afternoon with our hearts full. You have blessed our family beyond our wildest dreams. We're celebrating the first wedding anniversary of Aiden and Bailey and Matt and Emma. We are so grateful you have joined the Campbell family with ours. They are wonderful people and are a great addition to the family. We're also thankful for your hand in John and Vicki's lives and for all the positive changes you've helped them make. You have also blessed the family construction business. When Aiden and Matt expressed an interest in building houses someday, you found a way to make that happen. In addition to their own homes, they've already built several homes in town and will be building several more. With your blessings and guidance, JC's Hope is thriving and helping teenagers all around Hope. And, we recently learned that Josh and Amy are being blessed with another child. We could stand here all day and still not be able to count all our blessings. So, we ask humbly that you bless this food and the hands that lovingly prepared it. In Jesus's precious name, we pray. Amen."

And with his little spoon poised to dig into his food, Levi shouted, "Amen!"

~ The End ~